Nora and Alai
A.C.T.

She knows the truth.
It knows she has to run.

David Sines

First Printing, 2021

E-Book Edition ISBN-13: 978-1-7376942-0-5

Paperback Edition ISBN-13: 978-1-7376942-1-2

Hardcover Edition ISBN-13: 978-1-7376942-2-9

This is a work of fiction. Names, characters, places, and incidents either are the product of the author's imagination or are used fictitiously, and any resemblance to actual persons, living or dead, businesses, companies, events, or locales is entirely coincidental.

To all the friends and family that assisted in the creation process,

Thank you.

Prologue

Mom's necklace glitters from the sunlight coming through the window of the restaurant. I'm thrilled with how much she likes it. A nice lady gave it to me when we were buying presents.

"Nora, you can't invite strangers to the house," she says, eyeing the waitress walking away.

"Why not?" I ask while I scribble with a blue crayon.

She hesitates, "People can be mean."

"Was she mean?" I ask, switching to the green crayon to draw mom's hair over the blue.

Our waitress is pretty. I didn't realize she was mean. Mom knows everything.

A weird noise by the table catches my attention, and all the commotion in the restaurant begins to hush. I look across the table, and Mom is gone.

To the side, the mean waitress is crouching over something on the ground.

I don't know what's going on, but I'm scared. Where's Mom? Why is everyone quiet?

My lip quivers. I need to find Mom. I slide off my booster seat and instantly recognize my mom lying on the floor.

The waitress is talking, but I don't know what she's saying. I run over and push her away. She fumbles back.

"Get away from her!"

I pick up mom's hand to try and help her up. It feels heavy. Someone behind tries pulling me away by my arm, but I yank it free and kneel at mom's side.

Shaking her, she still doesn't wake up. Mom's necklace shifts on her chest — the skin is a scary white where it was resting.

In his bedroom, Howard kneels beside the bed. His wife lays limp on it. His breathing quickens, and his eyes go wide with adrenaline. He's seen death enough to know it at sight. But he is used to seeing it as it happens.

He pulls out a note he wrote during the night in his car — an apology note. He regretted the things he said before leaving. He always regretted something it seemed.

Taking his wife's hand, he wraps her fingers around the note before resting it on her chest. His knuckles feel something hard through the sheet.

Curious, he pulls the linen down to peer at what it is. He immediately recoils and gets to his feet. The sheet drapes over her hand, revealing pale dead flesh surrounding a gold pendant.

Howard recognizes it on sight for what it is. *Where did she get that?* She was not the brightest person, but she wasn't stupid.

A creak by the door alerts him to his daughter standing in the doorway. He sighs, and his mouth twists in contempt for her. *The one time she wakes up at a decent hour, and it has to be today. I suppose I should just tell her. But how?*

He turns to face her. She rolls her eyes and mutters something under her breath.

"Your mother's dead," he says sullenly.

"What!" she shrieks.

She stomps across the room and halts a pace from the bed, covering her mouth as she gasps.

Rounding on Howard, she points fiercely, "Why does she have that? Did you give it to her?"

Howard gives his daughter a level stare.

"I'm not an idiot. She must have found it somewhere and didn't recognize it."

"Liar!" she pounds his chest with her fist. "You knew it was there and gave it to her!"

"What are you talking about?"

"It's all your fault!"

She hits him again, and Howard snatches her wrist before she storms away.

He gives her a discerning gaze as she weakly attempts to pull free. His eyes widen at what he realizes.

"You knew it was there," he says.

His daughter meets his eyes and makes the poor choice of speaking.

Her voice is bitter ice. "It wasn't for her."

Howard loosens his grip in disbelief, letting his daughter break free and leave.

He steps over to the wall, his knees weak.

My daughter is a murderer, and it's my fault.

Taking her place in the center of her audience, Nyah begins, "You've all been selected to be part of a project that will require one thing. Your life."

The crowd stirs a little, and Nyah continues, "This is not a job you can walk away from. If you choose to stay, you stay for life. Due to recent catastrophes, as most of you are intimately familiar, humankind is failing itself. This project could prevent future terrorism and much more. But if anyone feels they cannot commit without reserve, you must leave now. This is your last chance."

People murmur among themselves for a minute, but no one moves toward the exit.

"Very good." Nyah then carefully draws out a chain from a box behind her. At the end of it, a golden star pendant dangles like a poisonous spider at the end of its web. She lifts it for all to see, catching gasps from those in the room. "This holds the key to our success."

CHAPTER ONE

Reality

In line for a hot pretzel from the street vendor after school, I feel the person behind me pushing against my upper back with his bulging stomach. My eyes go distant. I'm looking at the people in front of me, but I don't see any of them. Instead, all I see is the large person behind me.

I want to give him the benefit of the doubt so I move a step forward. I lower my backpack to my side so I'm not pressing it into the woman in front of me. Maybe I'm panicking for no reason.

The man steps closer again. If I inhale, I know my back will touch him. I feel my hair being lifted and stroked. My heart sinks, and I am frozen stiff.

If I walk away now, maybe he'll stay here. I hold my breath and walk away from the food cart, lifting my backpack over my shoulder. I head down the street toward the bus stop. Dad told me to stop going down here. I'll never come here again. Please, oh please, don't be following me.

Pretending to look at something on a tree as I pass it, I casually look farther back at the pretzel stand. I catch a glance of a few people standing in line, but I don't see the large man anywhere. His absence from my sight is only slightly reassuring. He's not on my heels. That's good. I slow my pace a little. My calves are tight from the burst of speed-walking.

I suck in a long breath, and my teeth feel tainted by the smog of the city.

The bus stop is one block away. I can almost see it. My heart is pounding from the encounter with the large man. I want to run, but I feel compelled to remain outwardly calm.

The sidewalk is relatively busy with people today. No doubt because of the warm air. The winter was bitterly cold this year. People are glad to be outside again.

A black truck grabs my attention, going in the same direction as me. I realize it is slowing down because it is looking for a parking spot. I feel silly for being jumpy at traffic. I try driving one of my fingernails into my thumb to force myself out of my panic.

"Where are you off to in such a hurry?"

The words glue my feet to the ground. My head is screaming at me, but I can't focus on what it wants me to do. I look to my left in front of me. A large man is leaning against the black truck that drove by. His thumbs are planted in his pockets, making his arms frame his thick stomach.

"I was going to pay for your pretzel, one of those deluxe ones with chocolate and sprinkles." He moves his hand in the air like he is sprinkling them on right there. "How 'bout I give you a ride, and I'll get you something nicer on your way home?"

He comes toward me like we are old friends. His hair is thin and dark gray. A thick burly arm reaches gingerly to put a hand on my shoulder.

My thumb begins to throb from the pressure of my fingernail, still digging into it. This single slight distraction breaks me from my frozen stance, and I duck out of his reach and run.

"Hey! Come back here!"

I hear him rushing up behind me, and I know I can't outrun him. A door opens to my right. I bolt inside, pushing past a woman carrying a grocery bag.

Inside the small grocery store, I hit my feet against the floor as fast as I can, going all the way to the back wall. I turn the corner and stop, using the aisle to hide. A few of the customers down by the packaged deli meats turn and look at me curiously.

I try to catch my breath, straining to do so quietly. My heart is pounding in my chest so hard I can almost hear it. I peek around the corner at the door. The man is talking to one of the workers. I can't imagine why. He then walks toward the cash registers.

Sighing in relief, I carefully move my feet back down the aisle toward the entrance, watching the end of the aisle like a hawk for the man. Sticking close to the opposite side, I creep out slowly.

Beyond the registers at the far end, I spot him scouting out the perimeter of the store, walking out of sight.

A woman pushes a cart past me. Her young daughter is in the seat crying. The mother has a one-track mind and doesn't acknowledge her daughter's cries. I move faster to get to the door, and my foot kicks something soft.

A small pink unicorn glides to a stop on the scuffed tile floor. Looking down past the aisles, the man is nowhere to be seen. I glance at the girl crying and see she's looking at the toy on the ground. I snatch it off the floor and trot it over to push it into the girl's lap before running back the other way.

As I get close to the door, I take another look behind me. Walking from around the back, where I hid moments ago, is the man.

My heart races, and my arm is snatched by something before I can burst through the exit. My feet run ahead of me as my body is caught just before I fall to the ground.

"Hold on there. It's time to stop running."

Grasping my arm is a worker. His thin white hair says nothing of his grip on me. I stand up and yank as hard as I can to reach for the door—anything I can use to pull myself free.

"Let me go!"

"Not until your father can take you."

I stop and try to make sense of what he's saying. My father isn't here. What is he...?

"Thank you, sir," the big man says, getting close now.

"Don't mention it. You listen to your father now, miss. He only wants what's best for you."

"He's not my father!"

"Settle down. Let's talk about this at home."

"He's not my father!" I try hiding behind the worker since he still won't let go.

People are looking now that I'm shouting. I yell louder. Trying to draw as much attention as possible while using the old man as a shield.

The big man sighs. "I'll be waiting outside."

He walks out of the store and out of sight. I sag down onto the floor and start sobbing. The old worker lets go of me. I'm so emotionally drained, I can't think.

People are talking above me, and someone kneels next to me, attempting to console me by rubbing my back soothingly. One of them walks outside.

Blinking, I rub the tears off my face and see what's going on.

The old worker is much less self-assured now. His face is long and worried. Next to me on the ground is a woman. Her brown hair is short, framing her warm light-blue eyes. Another woman is standing above me, seeming to be a barrier between the old man and me. The woman that is standing is stocky with short blonde hair. She has a fist on her hip, her other hand is shaking a finger at the old man.

"You're okay. You're safe," a quiet voice says next to me. I turn to look at the woman kneeling beside me. "Was that man your father?" she asks.

"No," I sob, "I've never seen him before."

"Okay. Don't worry about him. You'll never see him again."

"Is he gone?" I'm so shaken. I hug my knees to hold myself still.

"Yes, someone just went out and checked. He left."

"Was it the father?" a rough voice asks. I look up to see the stocky woman turned more toward me now.

"No. She said she never saw him before."

The stocky woman faces the older man. "You get on the phone and call the police. Then, you apologize to this poor girl."

The man stammers, stepping back. He looks down at me. "I'm so sorry. He said his daughter was mad at him. I..."

"I said go call the police first," the woman reprimands him.

"Right away," he says, running to a register and picking up the phone.

"Idiot men," the woman scoffs, her gaze following the worker.

The woman kneeling next to me says, "My name is Sharon. What's yours?"

"Nora," I say.

"Thank you for not walking by like the others," the standing woman says to Sharon.

"Don't mention it," Sharon tells her.

"They're sending an officer over. Shouldn't take long," the older man says, walking up again.

"Can I go home, please?" I ask.

The stocky woman speaks down to me. "Honey, the police need to file a report for these kinds of things. If you don't, that man might try again. And the next girl might not be as lucky as you."

Time and space begin to feel thick and slow like everything has the solid fluidity of molasses. People continue to walk in and out as I sit. The two women stay next to me. The cash register beeps as items are passed over the scanner. There is intermediate punching of keys on the register too. The two women start small talk about where they're from and who they know. I don't pay attention to what they say any more than I notice the number of beeps and clicks of the cash register.

The world is solidly clear in a physical sense, but the sounds and feel of time are hazy and distant.

The old man is hovering nearby, rubbing his hands together nervously. He leans forward to look outside. On spotting the police car pulling up, he hastily stumbles around us to greet the officer.

The officer walks up to me. He is small and thin. His hair and beard are short and red. He reminds me of a leprechaun in a dark-blue outfit instead of a green one. Ignoring the others, he bends down on one knee and gives me a comforting smile.

"Hey, kid. I'm Officer Harris. I heard some guy was pestering you here. Can you tell me what happened?" He pulls a pad of paper and pen out of his shirt pocket.

After nodding, I tell him about waiting in line for a pretzel after school. The old man starts sliding away to help a customer, but the officer halts him with a firm command to stay put.

"So, after walking away, did the man follow you?" the officer asks, turning his attention back to me.

"I didn't think so. But then he got ahead of me in a black truck and tried to get me to go with him."

"That's good to know. You didn't happen to get his plate number, did ya?"

"No, officer."

"Did you notice what make it was?"

I scrunch my face in confusion. "What?"

"Was it a Ford, a Dodge, or Chevy?"

"Oh. Umm. No, I didn't. It was tall, though."

"Hmm. Okay. Better than nothing. So, is that when he chased you in here?"

"Yes. I tried to get out while he was walking around looking for me. But he," I motion to the old worker, "stopped me before I..."

"Now, hold on there." The old man steps forward, putting a hand up. "I had no idea what was going on. The man chasing her told me when he came in that his daughter was angry with him and hiding in the store."

"I will get to you in a moment, sir," Officer Harris rebukes. "What happened when you were stopped?" he asks me.

"The man came back and claimed to be my father. I started yelling as loud as I could that he wasn't, and then he said he'd be waiting outside."

"Did anyone go outside to see where he went?"

I look over at Sharon beside me, not sure of the details.

"A worker stepped out and said he didn't see him," Sharon answers for me.

"Okay." Harris jots a few more things on his notepad and looks at me again. "And what is your name, miss?"

"Nora."

"Last name?"

I bite my lip. I don't want my dad to find out. "Thompson," I lie.

Officer Harris smirks like he knows what I am thinking. "Where do you live, Miss Thompson?" He emphasizes the last name, showing his doubt.

"I... forget."

"Uh-huh," he says. "Well, we'll figure that out when I drive you home."

My heart sinks. I can't let him drive me home. Dad will ground me for sure. Plus, can I trust the officer? He seems innocent enough, but I've been wrong before. Horribly.

CHAPTER TWO

Diversions

Officer Harris stands up to address the old man.

"Do you have surveillance cameras? Never mind, I see them now. Can you show me the video recording?"

"Yes, officer," he says.

"Are you two nice ladies able to keep an eye on her till I get back?"

The stocky woman frowns.

"I can stay with Nora," Sharon answers. Then gesturing at the other woman, adds, "But I believe she has somewhere to be if she can go."

"Sure. I'll need your license and a phone number I can reach you at."

"Of course. Thank you. I wasn't going to say anything, but my son is coming home from military school tonight." The woman hands the officer her license and gives him two phone numbers to contact her if needed. She looks down at Sharon and shakes her hand before picking up a bag of groceries and says to Sharon, "Thank you. You take care."

"After you, sir," Officer Harris tells the old man. "We'll be right back, miss."

They walk down to the back and through a double-door behind the refrigerators.

Sharon sighs and curls her lip. "You doing alright?" she asks me.

I sniff. "I guess so."

Looking out through the windows, I watch the people go by as I think. There's got to be a way out of this. They have a camera. The officer shouldn't need me for anything more. Maybe I could ask Sharon for something and walk out while she's away. I ponder this—knowing my opportunity could be gone any minute—my heart races as I get ready to lie one more time.

"Sharon," I say as meekly as possible, "can you get me some water? I'm so thirsty."

Sharon picks her head up to look around. My heart skips a beat as I wonder if she will just ask someone else to get it.

"Umm. I'm not sure..." Sharon pauses, still looking. I'm relieved inside when I realize she's not searching for a person. She's looking for where to get the water. "I suppose I could just grab a bottle from the case over there. They probably won't mind. Yeah, I'll be right back."

Sharon gets up and starts walking toward a refrigerated display case about 30 feet away. I have only seconds to walk out. But it has to be perfect. I glance toward the back of the store. The officer isn't on his way back yet. Sharon is halfway to the case.

Sliding up quickly, I move to the door. I don't make a sound, and I don't draw attention to myself by running.

Outside I want to run as fast as I can. But I know it is too soon. I can't mess this up.

At the corner, I see a city bus slowing down near the intersection. Across the road is the bus stop. There's my reason to run. I'm just a kid trying to catch the bus before it leaves the next stop. I lock my eyes on the bus, and I begin jogging to the crosswalk.

Though the light is flashing red for crossing, I race through as it turns solid. I'm just a kid trying to get across before I get hit by a car, that's all—nothing unusual here.

The bus passes me and pulls to the side just ahead. I trot up behind two people, waiting to get on.

I can't help myself. I look behind me at the small grocery store. Sharon is standing on the sidewalk. She stands on her tiptoes, shielding her eyes from the afternoon sun with her hands. A bottle of water glitters in one of her raised hands as she moves. I crouch down, pretending to retie one of my shoelaces just as the bus door opens. Waiting until the last second, I stand and walk onto the bus.

At the back, I peer out to get a last look at Sharon. She's given up and gone back inside. I let out a relieved sigh as I sit down in an empty seat.

My body is still quivering from all that has happened. I dig out my phone and check the time, trying not to look like I'm rattling dice in my hand. Surprisingly, it is not that late. I should be able to make it home before my dad does. Judy might beat me there, but that's okay.

Drawing my backpack close to my chest, I hug it. It's a small comfort, embracing an inanimate object, but it feels so good right now. I let my eyes close as I listen to the sounds around me—the background noise of people on the bus shuffling, phones chiming or chirping, and the rhythmic thumps of the tires on the road.

Before long, though, I have to open my eyes again. The incongruous stopping, turning, speeding up, and slowing down starts to make me queasy. I feel so drained.

The lack of food, I realize, is what is making me feel sick. My hunger has returned fourfold—I never got my warm pretzel.

Idly I open my bag, searching for something to ease my stomach, even though I know nothing will be there. I feel like everyone is watching me, and I am grateful for any distraction—no matter how pointless.

The bus is getting full now. People are heading home for the day. An elderly couple hobbles onto the bus. I see them coming to the back, and I know I have the last empty seat beside me.

Standing up, I lift my bag over my shoulder and grab the rail. I gesture to them to take my place so they can both sit and be together. They look so sweet.

"Why, thank you," the elderly woman says.

The elderly man gives a big smile and nods. He sits down next to his wife, putting his cane between his legs, with his hands resting on the hilt.

The woman takes in her surroundings and then looks up at me. "Are you traveling by yourself?"

"Yeah."

The woman gapes. "You better be on your way home," she scolds.

"Don't be hard on her, Riley. If she's out on her own, I'm sure she can handle herself. Can't ya?" He gives me a wink.

"Don't encourage her, Mark. You know how bad things are." She opens her large purse and pulls out a small black cylinder. "Take this."

Gingerly I reach for it just as the bus hits a bump, and I knock it out of her hand. The woman hisses.

"Pick it up. Quick," she says.

It barely rolls on the floor before I grab it. Twisting it around in my hand, I read the label—pepper spray.

"You keep that with you wherever you go, you understand? Flip off that cap and spray the eyes of anyone trying to hurt you. And when you do, be sure to close and cover your eyes. Then run away." The woman shakes her finger at me like she is scolding her own child. She then folds her arms on her lap satisfactorily. "I've had to use it three times in my life. Saved my husband from getting his wallet stolen once. That's not counting the times I merely threatened with it."

"There was nothing in the wallet. It wouldn't have mattered," the old man interjects.

"It would so have mattered. If there was nothing in it, she would have stolen your fingerprints and framed you for murder or the like," the woman argues.

"Just cause it happened to one person doesn't mean it happens to everyone."

His wife scoffs at him. All the sweetness I had seen in her when they stepped on has shattered beyond repair within a few minutes. She's so pushy. I want to give the pepper spray back to her just to disagree with her.

"It's okay. You don't have to give me this," I say.

The woman keeps her arms crossed. "Nonsense. You have something like that already?"

"Well, no."

"I've got a whole pack of them in the apartment. You keep that. I'll get another out of the closet when we get home."

Thinking about my afternoon, I know it's a good idea. I don't know that I will ever walk the streets again alone, but you never know.

"Thank you," I tell her.

"See, Mark. This is a smart one. She knows it's a good idea."

Mark gives me an apologetic smile. I smile back like it's fine.

The last 10 minutes of my bus ride are filled with dos and don'ts. I'm exhausted from keeping my mouth shut and agreeing to everything the woman says. I'm amazed that her husband has been able to put up with it.

Getting off the bus, I think to myself, the next thing she would say is that forks are too dangerous to eat with. But the pepper spray was a good idea. She wasn't wrong about anything she said—exactly. Just a little dramatic about supposedly dangerous scenarios.

My house is two blocks away from the bus stop. I want to rush home, but I still feel like eyes are watching me. So, I walk as fast as I can without looking like I'm in a hurry.

Arriving at my house, I make sure to check the mail as I usually do. I don't want anything to indicate that I'm acting differently from any other day. Tucking the mail under my arm, I unlock the door with my key. My dad refuses to get a digital lock. He insists that old-school locks are just as safe and reliable.

The air inside is uncomfortably warm. I set the mail on the bench by the door as I take my shoes off. A glistening image of a large pizza is sticking out of the pile of mail—my mouth waters. I pick the mail up, take it over to the kitchen, and drop it on the counter for Dad.

I open the fridge. On the middle shelf is a cold, hard slice of pizza wrapped in plastic. I take it out and unwrap it. The smell of tomato and seasoning beckons me. I don't wait to warm it up. I start eating and take it upstairs.

Reaching my room, I stop to pull my socks off and drop them into the hamper next to the door. I wiggle my toes into the plush lavender carpet, letting it welcome me home. I set my bag down by my desk and sit down to look out the window as I finish my pizza.

The air is much better in here. I had left my window open from the night before. We live far enough from the center of the city that it is considerably fresher. We have trees around our neighborhood. We even have one in our backyard.

As I lick my fingers clean, I hear the chirps of baby birds out in the tree. I dry my fingers on my pants, feeling a little guilty that I was stuffing my face while they had to wait for their meal. They'd be fed soon enough, though.

The door opens downstairs. I can hear my dad talking on the phone. It kind of sounds like two people down there. While Dad is still speaking, I hear footsteps coming up the stairs. Judy. She shuts her bedroom door, and I can hear her talking on the phone now, too. She sounds excited about something.

Good. That should help distract Dad if I begin spacing out. I think once I get past this evening, I can put today behind me. Just a few more hours.

Downstairs I hear Dad in the kitchen with a pan. I usually help him with dinner, and I don't want him to wonder where I am. I need him to think I've been home and waiting for an hour.

Taking a deep, slow breath, I head back down.

My dad is pulling out ingredients from the fridge and cupboards. The island is half-covered with food. Looks like he stopped at the store on his way home. My stomach flips at the thought of a store.

He stands up straight as he turns around with a handful of tomatoes and an onion. His hair is dark and short, his beard only a little longer. Both are well-trimmed and styled. To the left of his eye is a crescent scar from a run-in with a mugger last year.

"Hey, honey. I was just wondering about you. Did you have a good day?"

Thankfully, he is looking at his phone when he asks. I go to the counter and grab a cutting board to distract myself.

"It was alright," I say, inwardly cringing at my weak voice.

"Everything okay?"

I don't look at him. I act like I'm trying to find something.

"Yeah. It's just been a long day. I'm tired."

"Oh. Sorry to hear that. Do you want me to take care of dinner?"

This is genuinely tempting.

"I'll be fine. What are we making?"

Dad is texting on his phone, and he takes a minute to respond. I feel so stupid as I look at the scar on his face. I know why he doesn't want me walking the streets near my school. I wonder if I might have ended up with a scar if the man grabbed me on the sidewalk. I try hard to push the thought out of my head.

"Uh, Mexican. Tacos. With all the bells and whistles." His smile is big and enthusiastic.

Blinking a few times, I snap out of my daze. Scratching my head, I look up at him, bewildered. "That's a lot to do. We're going to have leftover tacos the rest of the week. Are you working overtime for the next few days?"

His phone chimes and he looks at it before answering. His smile turns to a frown. I wait for his answer, and the more I look at him, the more I have a sinking feeling he knows something. He purses his lips and looks straight at me. He knows. Someone must have seen me at the store and is asking about me. Who? What does he know? These thoughts race through my head, chasing each other.

"Nora, we need to talk."

CHAPTER THREE

Surprises

My eyes fix on Dad warily, and I step over to a barstool to sit down. It feels like the right thing to do. I hold my tongue. He hasn't said anything, and I'm not going to blab about it. Maybe he just knows that I didn't take the school bus home. I have to stay calm.

Discreetly, though, I brace myself to be berated for anything and everything that happened this afternoon.

Dad's face then turns into a slight smirk. I'm baffled. What does he need to talk about? He opens his mouth, but it just hangs there a moment and clamps shut again.

Planting his hands on the surface of the kitchen island, he hunches his shoulders and looks up at me. I don't have to try and hide anything. I'm genuinely dumbfounded and perplexed, wondering what is on his mind.

"You know I loved your mother," he says finally.

"Okay," I say cautiously.

"No one could ever take her place." He sucks in a breath. "But it has been six years, and I think we are all ready for a change. You and Judy are getting older, and you guys need... female input from time to time."

This is catching me so off guard that I can't quite grasp what he is saying. A female's input? Relaxing in my seat, I just blink at him—confused.

Dad licks his lips and grits his teeth.

"I'm seeing someone. We've been meeting for lunch quite often. I think you and Judy will really like her."

This hits me hard in my chest. Dating? My dad is dating? Why does he think we need another mother? We're doing fine. What 'input' could we possibly need that Dad can't give us?

"Why do you think Judy and I need this?" I say finally.

"Okay. You don't need it. It would be nice for you to have."

"You mean it would be nice for you to have." Crossing my arms, I glare at him.

"Hey, don't be like that. I'm thinking of all of us."

"Why haven't you told us this before? How long have you been dating?" My face is feeling hot.

"Well, I..." he scratches the back of his neck, "Okay, you got me there. I should have told you sooner. But you know how hard it is to find a decent, honest person these days. She just walked into the dealership one day looking for a car, and we hit it off. I didn't want to bring it up with you like this just to find out a week later that she is only after money or something. But she is a good person. Good for us, even."

"So then, you just invite your girlfriend to dinner before mentioning it to us?"

"I wasn't planning on telling you everything today. I was gonna have her come as a friend and just see how everyone got along first. But Lilly insists that I be upfront with you. She said if I didn't tell you both, that she wouldn't feel comfortable coming."

"Good. Don't tell Judy and tell this woman to forget it."

"I picked up Judy and told her on the way home. I was hoping that would suffice and that I'd wait to tell you. I'm sorry. I didn't mean for it to start off this way."

Blinking the tears out of my eyes, I sniff and walk away. I've heard enough. I just want to get away. Judy comes down and stops me at the steps.

"Hey, did Dad tell you?" Judy asks me.

I nod. She pulls me close and gives me a hug.

"It won't be that bad. Dad says she's really nice. Just pretend she's a friend coming to dinner and see how it goes."

Pushing her away, I go upstairs. I have nothing to say to her. I appreciate her kindness. We don't do much together anymore. But she is always nice to me. I stop on the stairs and ask her, "Can you help Dad with dinner tonight?"

"Sure, Nora. I'll let you know when to come down."

"Thanks."

Continuing up to my room, I shut the door and lay in my bed. I settle down on my back and stare at the ceiling. The ceiling is plain and flat. Whoever painted this room didn't do a good job. Specks of drywall are visible. Maybe a dozen of them.

Shutting my eyes, I try to just reason things out and think.

Can I let my dad date? Sure. It's not like I'm the one dating. What is the worst that could happen? She could be a serial killer and murder us in our sleep after they get married. Yeah. Wonderful thought, Nora.

Rubbing my forehead, I try to shut my mind down. I just need to lay here for a while and not think. Don't think.

A knock at the door startles me awake and sends my heart racing miles per second.

"What?" I say, trying to calm myself back down.

"Lilly is going to be here soon. Are you alright? I sent you a text." Judy's muffled voice comes through the closed door.

"You did? Oh, I guess I fell asleep."

Standing up, I saunter to the door and open it. Judy is leaning against the doorframe and pushes herself back as the door swings into my room.

"Did you take a nap?" she asks incredulously.

"I wasn't trying to," I yawn. "What time is it?"

I can tell from the sunlight coming through my window that it is almost dusk.

"Seven o'clock." She tells me. "Are you feeling okay?"

Running a hand through my hair, I yawn again.

"Yeah," I say, still yawning. "I'm not sick if that's what you mean. I didn't know I was that tired."

All the yawning causes my eyes to water a little, so I rub them dry.

"How are you feeling about tonight?" she asks.

"I don't know. Fine, I guess." I sniff, and my voice begins to break a little. "I miss Mom."

"Oh, Nora, come here."

Judy hugs me close and walks me to her room. We sit on her bed, and she leans back to push a strand of hair out of my face. A tear runs down my cheek, and I wipe it off.

"Having someone else here feels so wrong, Judy. How can Dad even think of dating?"

"Dad isn't trying to replace Mom. He's just looking for another friend to share his life with. Someone that can help out around the house too." She rubs my shoulder.

"It won't be all bad. And maybe this won't even work out. So, let's not be too hard on them, okay?"

Nodding, I lean on Judy for a bit. It feels so good to be home and with my sister. She picks up her head.

"Just a sec," she says, getting up.

Judy goes to her dresser and opens a jewelry box. Rummaging around, she starts setting things out. Finally, she plucks a ring out and quickly tosses the other stuff back inside. She brings the ring to me and holds it out.

"This was Mom's. She gave it to me when I was seven."

I take the ring from her delicately. It is silver with a red stone set in it. Probably not worth anything, but it is pretty. The silver is bright and smooth. The red stone is translucent and makes a pentagon shape.

"It's beautiful," I say.

"You can have it. Wear it tonight. A little piece of Mom to have with you no matter what happens."

"Really? Thank you. You don't want it?"

She sighs. "I don't remember Mom the way you do. Maybe you were too young. I kept it cause I care. But since you might actually wear it, you might as well have it."

"Thank you, Judy." I stand up and give her a big hug.

Stepping back, I try it on. It's too big for my ring finger. I try it on the pointer of my right hand. Perfect. I smile at Judy, and she smiles back.

"I should go back down to let Dad know you're okay. You might want to change and freshen up." She gestures by waving her hand in front of her nose.

I realize that I must stink from the sweat of my short burst of running. Not to mention the stress. I nod graciously, and Judy runs downstairs.

After freshening up and putting on clean clothes, I head downstairs. Mom's ring glistens on my finger as I watch it sliding down the banister on my hand. I'm grateful that it isn't a necklace. Perhaps I'd wear a necklace if it was my mom's, but I'm glad it's not.

The aroma of Mexican food beckons me as I go down.

"Mmm. It smells amazing." My stomach flips as I remember we won't be enjoying the food alone.

"I fried the corn shells just the way you like them," my dad shouts from the kitchen. He peeks around the corner at me as I follow my nose to the food. He is wiping his hands off on a towel.

"Did you make guacamole too?" I ask him.

He grins at me. "Uh-huh." Dad gives me a sideways hug. "We good?"

"No." I scowl at him. "But I'll be good." I return the hug.

"Thank you," he says, then kisses me on the top of my head.

I grimace, hoping he doesn't smell sweat in my hair. I only used a washcloth to freshen up my skin. He doesn't seem to notice. Silently I thank the frying oil for the heavy aroma in the air.

"When is she supposed to be here?"

"Any minute now," he replies. "She stopped at a store to pick up mangos."

"Why mangos?"

"She said it's for the tacos."

"Doesn't that sound amazing?" Judy pipes in.

"Sounds interesting. I'm not sold on it, though," I say stubbornly.

"Don't forget, you promised to be a good sport about this." Dad points his finger at me. "Lilly is looking forward to meeting you. Be nice."

Hearing the doorbell ring, my body tenses. She's here. What am I supposed to do? This is going to be so awkward and annoying. I panic briefly, wondering if she was at the same grocery store that I was at. I dismiss it, though. Even if it was somehow the same one, it couldn't have been at the same time.

My thumb brushes against my mom's ring, and I squeeze it tight as if I'm embracing a mini version of my mom's hand.

Dad raises his brows excitedly and looks at my sister and me. "Ready?"

"Yes."

"No."

My sister elbows me. "Yes," I grumble.

Dad walks to the door and takes a deep breath before opening it.

On our cement deck is a tall, fair-skinned woman with red curly hair. Her figure is slender and softly defined.

If she had been short, I might have thought she was the sister of Officer Harris. I'm sure there's no relation, though.

My gut instantly tells me that she is devious and evil. Just look at that sweet face. No one is that sweet. She's pretending to be something she's not and using her looks to... well, I don't know what. But I am convinced she's up to no good.

CHAPTER FOUR

Invaded

"Hi, ya'll," Lilly says, lifting a produce bag in triumph. "I got the mangos."

Her smile is contagious, which is downright annoying. I keep my face flat and unresponsive.

"Hi, Lilly," Dad says. He hesitates to lean forward, and I raise an eyebrow at him. Awkwardly, he welcomes Lilly with a half-hearted hug.

"So," Lilly says, "these are your precious children. Let me guess. You're Judy, and you must be little Nora. Oh, Jett, they are simply adorable."

My face heats at her diminutive mannerism. Little Nora? Maybe I should call her red-mop-Lilly. The thought makes me smile.

"It's nice to meet you, Lilly." Judy offers a hand.

"And very nice to meet you, Judy." Lilly takes her hand and shakes it limply, then reaches out for mine. Inwardly, I recoil, but I take her hand. Her palm is smooth and uncomfortably warm.

"Let me take those from you. C'mon in. Judy, would you wanna show her around, maybe?" Dad says.

"Sure, Dad."

Dad takes the mangos from Lilly, and Lilly steps inside.

"Y'all want me to take my shoes off?" she asks, glancing down at the shoes by the door.

"Yes, please," Judy tells her.

I stand off to the side with my arms crossed, watching her slip out of her high heels. She stands up tall and smiles.

"What a quaint house," she says, looking around. "My daddy and I lived in a big house in Texas. Probably twice the size of this. You know what they say, we like things big in Texas." She laughs, then steps into the living room with Judy.

Rolling my eyes, I follow them grudgingly. Judy gives me a stern look while Lilly inspects a picture on the wall. I uncross my arms and stick my hands in my pockets to try to appear more peaceful. But I get bored and go plop on the couch.

"Is this little baby Nora?" Lilly croons.

"Yep. That's Mom holding her hand."

"Aww. So sweet. I am sorry for your loss. Your daddy told me the story. Absolutely tragic. One of my cousins died from that too."

"Thanks," Judy says. "Sorry about your cousin. Were you two close?"

"Nah. She was kind of a snob. Still, it was sad." She begins looking at the other pictures. "Oh. That must be your mom there. Very pretty."

I can't stand to hear them talking about Mom, so I get up and walk away. Judy spots me from the corner of her eye. She doesn't say anything.

In the kitchen, Dad is cutting up the mangos and putting them in a serving dish. I grab some plates and take them to the table. I hear Judy and Lilly speaking faintly. I try to listen as I set the table, but I can't make out what they're saying. Their quiet tone makes me suspicious.

Dinner soon commences, and Lilly makes us all put pieces of mango on our tacos. Dad and Judy are practically giddy at how good it is. When I take a bite, my mouth waters before my teeth break through the surface of the soft fried corn shell. The oil, salt, and spices dance in my mouth.

Instantly though, the dance is bombarded by the sweet mango. I take note of the fresh sweetness. It is an unwelcome visitor.

"Sorry, I think I prefer mangos on their own," I say, and I start picking off the remaining pieces from my taco.

"Oh. That's alright, hon. I suppose it's not for everyone." Lilly waves her hand dismissively. "Judy, you have to come by the store sometime. I get a discount. It's still pricey, but I'm sure we can find something for you in the clearance section. There's always enough there to fill an empty barn."

"That'd be awesome. I love La Manière's. My friends and I go in there to window shop once in a while. I wonder if I've seen you there."

"Prob'ly not. I only work the weekday shifts."

Lilly takes another bite of her taco. The juice from it drips onto her chin, marring her perfect face. She quickly dabs it with a napkin.

I'm the only one solely focused on eating. I listen to them idly as they talk over dinner. Being the first one to finish, I go to the kitchen, intending to start cleaning up.

I find myself getting frustrated at the mess my dad and sister made. I prefer to clean up as I cook. They do not. The result was such a mess that I cannot comprehend where to even begin.

Dad leans back and says to me, "Nora, you don't have to worry about cleaning up. I'll take care of it."

The thought of Dad being occupied with cleaning dishes instead of talking to Lilly is enough to motivate me to push past my irritation and deal with the dirty, cluttered kitchen. The rest keep talking while I load the dishwasher. They don't appear to even realize I never replied.

After taking care of the dishes and the counters, condensing the mess to only leftovers, and a couple pans in the sink that didn't fit in the dishwasher, I wash my hands of it. Literally and figuratively.

Moving to the couch, I sit down and put my back to the arm of it. I make sure to face them—Lilly in particular. I keep Lilly in my sight and kick my feet up to get comfortable.

I pull out my phone and open all the apps that have notifications. My uncle Leo texted me. He likes to check on me often, especially since Mom died. There are a couple posts from kids at school that I glance over. Nothing is very interesting.

Looking up, I catch Lilly watching me while Dad and Judy are intent on their conversation. Lilly immediately pretends like she was casually viewing her surroundings. I watch her closely with my head down toward my phone, hoping she'll think I'm just a little girl glued to her social media.

Sure enough, I can tell she's looking at me again. She stops, though, whenever Dad or Judy starts talking to her. Soon she begins telling her stories of Texas and some wild things that happened at the boutique she works at.

Putting down the phone, I act like I'm very interested in what she says. But I'm more interested in what she does. I watch for any sign of unusual behavior. The only thing I spot is that she checks her phone repeatedly after Dad takes her empty plate away. So often that I try timing her. Two minutes. Five minutes. Three minutes. Seven minutes. I conclude there isn't a pattern. I can't think of why there would be one, but I don't want to miss anything.

It's almost ten o'clock, and Lilly's phone vibrates. She picks it up and frowns as she begins to type a message.

"Everything okay?" Dad asks her.

"Oh, nothin'. Don't worry about it, Jett. My roommate is just asking for the apartment to herself tonight."

"Where does she expect you to go?"

"I'll go stay at a hotel. I spent a month in hotels when I moved here. I know which one I like."

"That's ridiculous." Dad is sounding ticked off. "She should spend the night out if she wants privacy."

"Aw, you're so sweet. No, darlin'. She doesn't have the money. It's alright. I told her I could if she needed me to."

Dad sits back in his chair, his hands fixed on his hips, looking frustrated.

Judy starts fiddling with her napkin on the table. I see her eyes dart to me for a split second, then stare at the napkin in front of her. Lilly's phone vibrates again, and she starts texting back.

Don't you dare offer it, Judy. I try to will her to hear me by glaring hard.

"Dad, we do have the spare bedroom," Judy says timidly.

I clench my free hand. What is Judy thinking? We can't trust Lilly to stay the night. I wait in stillness to see what Dad will say. Lilly looks up from her phone and takes a moment to process what Judy said.

"Nah. Don't you worry about me either, pumpkin'. I'm not gonna intrude on your humble abode. Not yet, anyway." She laughs and gives Judy a wink.

"She has a point, Lilly. It seems silly to make you stay in a hotel when you could just stay here," Dad says.

I can't believe what I'm hearing. My dad, who tells me not to walk through town and doesn't let me or Judy have anyone stay the night, is telling Lilly, practically a stranger, that she can stay at our house.

"Jett, darlin', I hate to disagree with you, but I don't think you're thinkin' about everyone here."

Getting up from the couch, I walk up to the table and put my hands on the empty chair that I used during dinner. I look at my dad, perplexed.

"Dad, you don't even let Judy and me have friends stay the night. Are you really going to break your own rule, just because it's your friend?" I'm shocked at the words coming out of my mouth. But I hold my ground. Lilly is not going to stay here. Not if I can stop it.

"Nora, your friends don't have to pay for a hotel to find a place to sleep. Do you know how expensive hotels are?"

"Dad, it's not fair. You can't let her stay here," I protest.

"Excuse me," Lilly chimes in. "Ya'll are arguing for nothin'. I'm not staying here, and that's that. Jett, I appreciate your hospitality, but no. Nora, you are absolutely right. In fact, I think I may have overstayed my visit."

To my delight, Lilly stands up and sticks her phone in her handbag. Dad is speechless. Lilly leans over and kisses him on his forehead.

"Thank you for a nice evenin'. I've enjoyed getting to know your girls finally. I'll call you t'morrow." Turning to Judy, she pats Judy on the shoulder, giving her a warm smile, and walks around to me. She stands straight and respectful and sticks her hand out to me. "It's been a pleasure, Nora. Good job keeping your daddy in check. I hope we can get to know each other better in the future."

Hesitating, I take her hand and shake it. Dad opens his mouth to say something, but Lilly gives a commanding gesture to be silent. She walks down the hallway and gets her heels back on. The three of us follow to the door. Dad slips on a pair of shoes and steps outside with her.

When the door shuts, Judy whips around to face me. "What was that all about, Nora?"

"Me? Why did you offer the spare bedroom in the first place?"

"Because it was the nice thing to do. Dad has been dating her for months. Do you think she'd even be in our house if he didn't trust her?"

"Months?" I ask quietly.

Judy's face softens. "I thought you knew."

"He left that part out," I mutter. I'm not sure what I think of that little tidbit of information. I wonder if he left that out on purpose or not. "Anything else I should know?"

Judy avoids my eyes and starts rubbing her arms. She stares at the floor—thinking.

The sound of crickets wax and wane as the door opens and shuts again. Dad stands there, looking down at me. He remains quiet and decides to ignore me. Taking his shoes off, he announces he's going to bed.

"Go talk to him and apologize," Judy demands in a whisper.

"There's nothing to apologize for. Lilly didn't want to stay anyway."

Judy gives me a level look. "Go apologize, or I'm going to tell him you didn't take the school bus home today."

CHAPTER FIVE

Perception

Keeping my face calm, I try not to panic. But inside, my heart is racing. What does Judy know? She can't know about all that happened, can she?

"How do you know that?" I ask.

She smirks at me. "A wise sister doesn't reveal her sources."

Heading to the kitchen, she looks over her shoulder at me. She appears very pleased with herself. Did she really know, or did she just make a guess, and I slipped with my reply?

I stand there debating about pushing her further. But I conclude that the best course of action is to assume she knows nothing. If I hounded her with questions, she'd know something was up and reverse the questioning to me. Or worse, tell Dad anyway.

Up the stairs, Dad's bedroom door is open. I can hear a newscast report from inside. I knock softly.

"You can come in," he calls.

Pushing the door open further, I step in. Dad is sitting on the bed with a pillow propped up against the back. He's already changed into something more comfortable. He's wearing a loose blue T-shirt with red plaid pajama pants. He has a leg bent up to support his elbow as he watches the news report on his phone. Glancing in my direction, his frown deepens. A tap on the screen pauses the video and he puts the phone down, sitting up straighter as I approach.

"What is it?" he asks.

"I came to say I'm sorry."

"Sorry for what?" He watches me expectantly.

"Sorry I spoke up like that."

Dad just sits there waiting for more. I sit down on the end of his bed.

"I'm sorry for how I acted about Lilly staying the night. But it really wouldn't have been fair."

"Do you think I'd do something that wasn't fair?"

"No," I grumble.

"If I decide to do something that you think is unfair, you can talk to me in private. Not in front of our guest."

"What should I have done differently, Dad? Should I have walked up to you and said, 'Dad, can I please talk to you in private for a moment?'" I ask mockingly.

"That's exactly right."

I sit quietly and think over what he's telling me.

"Okay, Dad."

"Good. Apology accepted." Dad relaxes a little and picks up his phone again. "So besides wanting to kick her out of the house, what did you think of her?" He holds his phone, ready to do something, but he waits for my answer.

"I... I don't trust her," I say, finally.

"How come?"

"She kept looking at me after dinner when she thought I wasn't watching."

Dad lifts an eyebrow.

"And I think she knew her roommate was going to text her. She was checking her phone constantly," I add.

Dad just shakes his head.

"You need to stop being so suspicious. Not everyone has ill intentions."

I know what he's alluding to. It makes my throat tighten to remember it, and I feel the water around my eyes.

"It's not that," I say. "I just don't trust her."

Dad nods, though he still looks doubtful.

"If I had any doubts about Lilly, I wouldn't have invited her tonight. We've been seeing each other for almost a year." He puts the phone down again and puts his legs to the side, dangling them off the bed like mine. "Nora, I love her. It would mean a lot to me if you try to see past these suspicions of yours."

My body convulses at this revelation. Love?

"What?" I'm suddenly standing, though I don't recall getting up. "You love her? Let me guess, you got eloped too and forgot to mention it. Try bringing us in the loop before you start falling for people, will you?"

I storm out of the bedroom just as Judy is walking down the hallway. She presses herself against the wall to get out of my way as I stomp into my room and slam the door.

CHAPTER SIX

Stiff and Lenient

I awake in a tired but decent mood. My dreams were about pushing Lilly out of the house. Every time she came back, and every time I chased her out. One time I chased her down the road and to the next town. That had been the last one, I think. A satisfying conclusion to the dream series 'Getting rid of Lilly.'

However, my stomach turns to rock when I realize no one else will share my feelings about these dreams. I'm forced to keep them to myself.

I don't want to head down for breakfast yet. I need more time to myself before facing Dad and Judy after last night.

Habitually checking my phone, I look at the text from Leo I got yesterday. He's inviting me to come and visit for a while. They've got a big event coming up at work related to the project he's been working on for years. So, I'd actually be able to see where he works. I enjoy visiting him. He's not married, so it's not that different from being home. It's just another house with more takeout and ice cream.

The idea of leaving is appealing and nerve-racking. I'd love to get away, right now especially. But what stupid thing would Dad do next with Lilly? I shudder at the thought of them getting even fonder of each other in my absence. I write uncle Leo back saying I'd have to think about it. I'd need to request time away from school before giving a definite yes, anyway.

At last, I feel that I have disconnected myself from the drama long enough to face it again. I look out the window for a moment, enjoying the peaceful Saturday morning from my bedroom. My gut tells me this is just the calm before the storm.

Leaving my bedroom, I see from the open doors that Dad and Judy are awake, as I suspected.

Trotting down the steps, I can hear at least one person eating at the table by the soft clang of silverware on a bowl or plate. The vinyl flooring feels cold to my bare feet as I reach the bottom.

Judy stops eating her cereal when I walk in. She glowers at me from over her bowl. I ignore her mood and grab a toaster pastry out of the freezer. I feel my body tensing from her resonating attitude as I rip the packaging open. I keep my actions controlled and gently slide the toaster lever down until it locks.

"Where's Dad at?" I ask without looking at Judy.

"He needed some time to himself to think. So, he's walking around the block till he sorts out what to do."

"What to do? What to do about what?"

Judy slams something onto the table. I whip around to face her and see her hand in a fist inches from her cup. Her intense eyes scream at me as she speaks through clenched teeth.

"What to do about your attitude."

I scoff and roll my eyes. I tried to be casual. If Judy won't do the same, I don't want to be a part of it. I grab a glass for some orange juice.

"Do you have any idea how much your words cut at him? He found someone to fill a void in his life. How can you be so heartless?"

Keeping my mouth shut, I take the juice out of the refrigerator and pour myself a glass. Judy doesn't accept the silent treatment. She just gets up and stalks over to me. She leans against the counter with her arms crossed, looking straight at me. I don't meet her eyes.

"What if it was you, Nora? What if you found something that brought a little more meaning to your life? Would you like me or Dad to scold you and say it's not fair?" Judy then performs a mock imitation of the scenario, "Nora, you can't do that. It's replacing your mother, and that's not allowed."

Without thinking, my hand flies up and strikes Judy across the face. My heart races, and I am bewildered by what I just did. I keep my eyes fixed on Judy, though. She was surprised too, but it was only for a second. She looks down at me like an icy queen addressing a lowly servant.

"You know that's what this is about as much as I do," she says. "Dad doesn't need permission to be happy. So, stop acting like a baby and try to be happy for him."

Judy picks up the glass I just poured and takes it for herself. Leaving her bowl and cup at the table, she takes the juice upstairs. Leaving me alone.

I sag into the closest chair and quake after the verbal onslaught. Nervously, I pull my hair over my shoulder and run my fingers through it. The toaster pops, but I don't even care. The hair running through my fingers is a little soothing, but my appetite is gone. I can't remember a time that Judy was ever that stern with me. I don't think anyone has. It shook me to my core.

The click of the front door's lock, followed by the swish of the door opening, alerts me to Dad coming back home. I sniff and stand up, resuming the preparation of my breakfast. The pastry isn't warm, but I put it on a plate anyway. Getting another glass, I pour more OJ. I take a deep, slow breath before Dad comes to the kitchen.

As I sit down with my breakfast, Dad makes his way to the cupboard and gets out a granola bar. I go through the motions of eating. The pastry is tasteless today.

Dad sits down at the other side of the table. Half his bar is gone, and he chews, appearing to contemplate what to say. I keep my head down and stare off into the air next to the table as I eat.

"Do you want me to break things off with Lilly?" he asks calmly.

I still don't look at him. My gut is twisting inside, so I refrain from taking another bite. I don't know what to do with myself. I rub my hands along the pant legs of my fleece pajamas. I can't bring myself to say anything.

Judy's words ring in my head, along with my own thoughts. I shake my head 'no.'

Dad settles back in his chair, and I find it easier to look at him now. His face is expressionless.

"Are you sure about that?"

I swallow hard and say, "I don't like any of this, but I don't want you to call things off because of me." I feel my mom's ring on my finger, and I run my thumb over the stone.

"Thank you, Nora."

Nodding, I get up and walk over to him. He pushes his chair back, and I sit on his lap, wrapping my arms around him. He holds me close.

Aware of the ring still, I intentionally press it closer than the rest of my hand, letting Mom be a small part of this moment. I can't decide if the moment is good or bad. But we are here together, and that's all I care about right now.

CHAPTER SEVEN

Merciful and Suspicious

The following week I am pushed to my limits with
Lilly. Nearly every night since Friday, Lilly is over at
our house. Sunday evening, she came with bags of
clothes from La Manière's, insisting that I try on a
dozen different things.

"Don't bother looking at the price tag. It's marked
down from that, anyway. It's a gift from me to you.
Anything you don't want, I'll just return when I go to
work in the mornin', alright?"

Whenever I was tempted to give a rude reply, I
would catch Judy giving me an icy stare that shut my
mouth. Everything Lilly had me try was too big. It
made me wonder if she thought I was fat.

Tuesday and Wednesday, she brought food from my
favorite restaurants. The night before each, I was cross-
examined by Dad and Lilly to find out what my
favorite foods were.

When I would look at Lilly, I didn't want to
cooperate. Her eager eyes would sparkle as she'd gaze
at me expectantly. Dad then would stand beside her

and offer his opinion of what I would order. When I looked at him, I had to answer something, so I did. Usually agreeing with him.

Those interrogations resulted in me eating takeout, with Lilly bouncing in her seat with every bite I took. Judy gave me a smug look at each meal. Dad only seemed to notice the delight on Lilly's face.

It's been five days, and the giddy chemistry between Dad and Lilly is more than I can stand. I want to gag at how happy they are all the time. Compared with their goofy grins, getting the cold shoulder from Judy is preferable.

It's Thursday night, and I have not taken up uncle Leo's invitation. I can't decide, so I keep pushing off a decision. I check with Dad, and he has the gall to have me ask Lilly if she cares.

Judy's ears pick up on the name Lilly, even as she is talking with her.

"What's that, Dad?" she asks him.

"Oh, I was talking to your sister. She was asking about visiting your uncle Leo, and I said she should check with Lilly too in case she has something planned."

I look over at Judy. I can see the sinister delight hidden in her face.

"You can ask her now, Nora," Judy says, without a hint of mockery. "I forget what I was talking about anyway."

I doubt she really forgot. She should be an actress. Her performance is spotless. I try not to grit my teeth.

"Lilly," I say, "would it ruin any of your plans if I leave for a week?"

"Of course not, darlin'. You go right on ahead. Go have an adventure."

It occurs to me that this is sealing the deal. That I am going and taking the only resistance to their union with me. Can I back out? Is that what I want?

"Well, I don't know for sure yet if that's what I'll do. It's just something I'm thinking about," I add casually.

Lilly sits quietly for a minute while the rest of us resume eating. I see her purse her lips and look over at Dad.

"Jett, do you think it would be a good idea for Nora to leave? Is it safe where her uncle lives? He's the one in D.C., right? You know how quick a riot can start there."

"She'd be just as safe, if not safer. He has a government salary and lives in a really good neighborhood. State-of-the-art security at the house, too." He takes another bite of pepper steak and fried rice. "I thought I mentioned that before," he says with his full mouth.

"That sounds nice," Lilly says in a smooth voice. "Maybe she should go then. It might be refreshing."

The smooth, drawn-out voice of Lilly sounds odd. She's up to something. I act disinterested as I take a drink of my water. Dad stops chewing for a second and looks directly at Lilly. I set my glass down, place the chopsticks delicately in my hand, and poke at a pineapple covered in sweet and sour sauce. Dad starts chewing again, still looking at Lilly, like he's trying to puzzle something out.

Judy is doing much the same as me. I can tell from her silence that she's intrigued too. It's not like her to be quiet. I suppose that's an advantage to my personality. I'm always quiet, so people can't tell if I'm listening or not paying any attention. At least, I hope I'm not being as apparent as Judy.

The table gets eerily quiet. For a while, all that is heard is the methodical chewing of food, glasses being set down on the table, and the soft thopps of chopsticks making contact with the plates. It begins to make Lilly fidget in her seat. She keeps looking at Dad. I can't figure out why she doesn't just say something herself if it makes her so uncomfortable. But I relish in the thought of her discomfort.

The sweet and sour chicken tastes delightful as the flavors burst in my mouth.

"Judy, how's your friend Melissa doing?" Dad asks.

I smirk behind my glass. Dad must have given up trying to interpret Lilly's silent communication.

"Do you mean, Mandy?" Judy replies.

Dad scrunches his forehead, thinking. "The one with the brain tumor."

"That's Mandy, Dad. She's fine. The surgery went well."

"Who's Melissa then?"

"I honestly don't know, Dad. You tell me," Judy laughs.

Dad smiles. The crescent scar by his brow straightens out from the wrinkle created by his grin.

The topic of a brain tumor causes Lilly to gush out with her own story of a cat in Texas that had a tumor on its neck. The details paint the mental picture of a ratty-looking cat with half a neck, flesh completely exposed and throbbing for weeks after surgery.

My appetite is now gone. I don't even want to look at what is left on my plate with red goo smeared all over it. I pick up my plate and take it to the trash, where I scrape off the last portion of food into the receptacle.

"Did my story upset you? I'm sorry, hon," Lilly says from the table.

"Yeah. It's okay. I was almost done anyway."

I place the plate in the sink and walk by the table toward my usual spot on the couch. Judy is poking her food around her plate. Lilly's story must have bothered her too a bit. We haven't been on the best of terms this week. But I love Judy regardless.

"Hey Judy," I say, "do you remember the time that park ranger asked Dad if we dumped?"

The smile on Judy's face stretches from ear to ear, and her eyes brighten. "Yes! Oh man, that was so funny."

"I bet Lilly hasn't heard it yet."

Dad groans behind me. I see Lilly, out of the corner of my eye, leaning forward anxiously waiting to be told all the details.

Judy begins her story with the rental of a camper for our trip to Arkansas. She's trying to keep herself from laughing as she talks. It's almost as comical just to watch her try to tell it as it is to hear it.

"So, before we leave, Nora and I need to use the bathroom one more time, right? Then as we are leaving, one of the park rangers stops us and asks Dad, 'did you...'" Judy starts snorting hysterically, "'did you... did you dump?' Hahaha!" She tries pulling herself together for the last line. "Dad just looks so confused, and he turns to us and says, 'I don't know, did you?'" Judy laughs and snorts again. "Dad thought he was asking if we took a dump in the bathroom!" Judy manages to say, wiping the tears off her face as she laughs.

"The ranger was referring to dumping the waste from the trailer. He wanted to make sure we paid the fee if we did," Dad clarifies.

Lilly laughs along with Judy. Even Dad can't help himself and starts chuckling.

Sitting down on the couch, I listen to them from the living room. I can't help but smile when Judy finishes her tale, and not because of the humor. When Judy is mostly done laughing, she promptly picks up her chopsticks and eats the rest of her princess chicken. Mission accomplished.

Lilly leaves for the night, and Judy gets in the shower before bed. Dad and I are doing a few last things in the kitchen before turning in. Dad is checking on our coffee maker, making sure there are enough coffee beans in the canister for it to grind and water in the reservoir.

For the first year of that coffee maker grinding at 5:30 AM every day, it would startle me awake. I am finally used to it enough that I'm at least not shaking like a frightened puppy anymore, even if it does wake me.

I look in the cupboard for what easy snack I want in my backpack for tomorrow. Reaching in, I move stuff around. I peer into the back corners, trying to find my favorite, chocolate-covered pretzels. But all I see are candy bars and chips. I take a bag of barbecue chips as a substitute.

"Can we get more of the chocolate-covered pretzels, Dad?"

He lifts his head up and bangs it on the open cupboard door.

"Ow. Ugh." He rubs the top of his head, messing up his nicely done hair. "Um, sure. Why don't you add it to the list? Or, you know what I mean, just put it in the cart for our next order on the app."

"Thanks," I say as I use my phone to add it.

"Oh, Nora, I was thinking about you going for the week. I think you should go. You've been super around here, with Lilly and everything. You deserve some time to yourself."

Putting my phone down, I consider what he's telling me. He sounds really sincere. Like he actually wants me to have a break from things. It puts my mind at ease about going.

"Okay, Dad. Thanks. I'll make sure to get what I need from school tomorrow."

Dad nods. "Sounds like a plan. I'll let Lilly know that I'll be driving you over Saturday." He walks over and kisses the top of my head, putting a hand on my shoulder. "Good night, Nora."

As Dad walks away, I get a sinking feeling now that I've committed myself to go. The empty room gives me an unusual chill. I shiver.

Remembering the conversation during dinner, I can't help but wonder. How much of this was Lilly's doing? The thought gives me a sick feeling in my stomach.

CHAPTER EIGHT

A Getaway

Saturday morning, we eat breakfast on the road. The drive to uncle Leo's place is about three hours if traffic is good. It has taken us three and a half because of the hard rain. It's just Dad and me in the car. Judy didn't feel like sitting for hours. I don't blame her.

We pull up to uncle Leo's house. It's a medium-sized bungalow with a mixture of different grays and a charcoal-black roof. Whoever designed it was a good architect. It looks like a piece of modern art made into a house.

The rain has stopped, though the clouds still look ominous. Opening the door, I feel the cool, damp air. It rolls into the car like an invisible cloud.

Upon getting out, I hear the heavy footsteps of my uncle walking through the shallow puddles of his walkway. Uncle Leo is tall. Like really tall. His hair is brown and curly. He has a thick mustache too. You might take him for a construction worker, or a lumberjack, from his physique. Though, are lumberjacks even a thing anymore? I don't know. But that would be a stereotype. In reality, he works at a government research facility. The only wood involved in his job is the desk he works at. That's my understanding, anyway.

Leo peeks around the corner of the garage like a shy little giant. He sees me and smiles wide. I wish he lived closer or even with us. I'd take him over Lilly any day.

"Hello, hello!" He waves—the motion of his arm looks odd because of his size. "Made it through that torrential downpour, I see. Did you have any trouble on the highway?"

"No. We had to drive slower, was all. It wasn't too bad," Dad replies.

"Can I help you with your bags?" Leo asks me.

"I just got the two. You can take the suitcase," I say.

Uncle Leo picks it up with ease. He points at it with his free hand.

"This is all?" he asks incredulously.

"Mhmm."

"I don't know that I could pack that light." He lifts it up and down, determining its weight, it seems. "Kudos on the bare necessities. C'mon in. Jett, you sticking around?"

"Just for a few minutes. I'd like to use your bathroom, do you mind?"

"You can run ahead of us if you need to," Leo says with a soft chuckle.

Dad and I follow him up the sidewalk by the garage to the house. I sidestep around the earthworms that have crawled out during the rain. The smell reminds me of fishing and makes me want to gag a little. I gratefully step off the sidewalk onto the deck.

Uncle Leo has a cement deck similar to ours. It is just a little nook in the building to offer shelter from the weather if need be—a brief refuge before getting indoors. It is completely bare. Leo doesn't care to decorate the outside of his home. Not much on the inside, either.

"Take your shoes off, please. I like to keep things clean rather than actually clean," Leo says as we walk through the door.

I remembered. Anyway, we take our shoes off at home too. Why he never remembers that I'll never know. The interior is modern and sleek. Hanging on the walls are a few large landscape paintings. Nothing extravagant. But the architecture makes up for the lack of decor.

"I'll take your bag to the spare bedroom." Leo then motions down the hall, "Bathroom is over there, Jett."

"Thanks," my dad says and then trots off.

I follow uncle Leo the short distance to the spare bedroom near the front of the house. The room is bright and plain, kept only for my sister and me when we visit. A simple double bed lays in the center with a shimmery dark-purple comforter. The carpet is firm and cream-colored. The walls are soft yellow, lightly contrasting with the white on the textured ceiling.

"Sometimes, I think of hanging a picture in here or something to make it homier," Leo comments, setting down the suitcase by the small closet.

"It doesn't bother me. It's not like I sleep with my eyes open."

"Haha. That'd be a sight. Come to think of it, a friend of mine did that, sleeping with his eyes open. Ugh. Makes my eyes go buggy just thinking about it."

My eyes are feeling odd, too, picturing that. I blink them a few times to reassure myself they don't have to stay open. Especially not all night.

"Well, I suppose the room will just stay as is then," Leo says and walks away.

Placing my backpack next to the bed, I go back to the main entrance. Dad is coming out already.

"Okay, I'm gonna get going. You call me if you need me to come get you," Dad says to me.

"Sure, Dad. I'll be fine, though."

"Have a safe drive, Jett. Thanks for dropping her off. Oh, and don't worry about coming to get her next week. I can bring her back."

"That'd be great, thanks. Have fun." Dad leans down and gives me a hug.

"Love you, Dad."

"Love you, Nora."

Dad opens the door, letting the stench of the earthworms waft in. It's just starting to sprinkle again outside. He quickly goes out in the rain, and I shut the front door.

"Did you have lunch yet?" Leo asks me.

"No."

"Well then, put on your shoes, and let's go." Leo grabs a light jacket hanging on a hook. "I've found a great new place I want to take you to."

In uncle Leo's old electric car, we make our way to downtown D.C. Thankfully I had a big breakfast, and I'm not starving. It takes us ten minutes just to find a suitable parking space. We see a curbside space by a fitness center and whip in to park.

Uncle Leo hands me an umbrella before we get out. It's bright pink with small rainbows printed all over it. I raise an eyebrow at him.

"Is there something I should know?" I ask facetiously.

"Do you have a problem with my choice in fashion?" he teases back. "Judy picked that out years ago when we got caught in a supermarket, and it started to rain. It's been sitting in here ever since."

"Ah. That makes more sense. And you think I want to carry around a toddler's umbrella?"

"It is not a toddler's umbrella. She was probably seven years old when she picked that out."

"Oh, well, in that case, do you want it?" I smirk at him.

"No, thank you. I wouldn't want people thinking I'm being rude to my niece, taking the only umbrella." He fakes a smile.

Sighing, I say, "Okay, but if I hear a snicker from anyone, I'm going to make sure the world knows it's your umbrella."

"Fair enough," he says and opens the car door.

Opening mine too, I step out and open up the umbrella. The rod, I see, is covered in glitter.

Leo goes to the parking meter and pulls out his tethered wallet. He gets a silver card out, inserts it into the meter, and then makes a few selections on the small screen. He looms over it with his tall body to block the rain as he tries to read the screen. I walk over and angle the umbrella for him. He nods somewhat appreciatively, then furrows his brows when he sees the glitter. I give him a knowing look, and he makes a few more taps on the screen.

"All set," he says.

"I didn't know they still made meters like that."

"It's not really that old. I remember when there used to be coin meters."

"Coins? Like currency coins?"

"Uh-huh. I still have some. I've been thinking about framing them."

We dance around the large puddles as we walk two blocks to the restaurant Leo is so adamant about going to. Through the hard rain, I see what looks like two potato chips with something wedged between them. The sign reads 'Chippers.' Leo pulls the door open and ushers me inside. Hugging the wall, I try to get around a crowd waiting for the rain to let up. Leo follows and is soon nudging me forward.

Past the crowd is a relatively short line of four people, which we file behind. I start looking at the menu, and I understand now what the picture was implying. Listed on the extensive menu behind the register are sandwiches. Next to each sandwich is a recommended potato chip that goes in the sandwich and on the side.

"The Asian Barbecue is excellent," Leo informs me. "They're all delicious, though."

I read through the menu. There are now only two people ahead of us. The line is moving quickly. I find a Monte Chipper, which looks to be their version of a Monte Cristo, with Alfredo Chips.

"You know what you want?" Leo asks me.

"Yeah, I think so."

There's only one person in front of us now, a thin woman in a burgundy raincoat. She pays for her food and takes a numbered plastic potato chip over to a table.

Just as the cashier greets us, a round woman with a giant hawk nose and broad-rimmed glasses cuts in front of us.

"I have been waiting thirty minutes for my sandwich." The woman throws the plastic chip in her hand at the cashier, striking him in the arm. She raises her voice. "I've asked you people four times about it. I demand to see the manager."

Leo and I take a step back from her. The cashier is rubbing his arm as he looks over his shoulder toward the kitchen.

"Just a moment, ma'am," he says dryly.

The woman stands there planted on the ground with her hands on her hips, glaring at the man's back as he walks away. She sniffs and pushes her glasses back up her large nose.

A second later, another man, wearing a tie, appears with the cashier. He steps to the end of the counter, motioning the woman to take a few steps down. She doesn't budge, though.

The cashier attempts to continue with our order while the manager negotiates with the irate woman.

"What can I get for you?" the cashier asks.

"Ma'am, I am sorry for the delay," says the manager. "Can I see your number, please, and I will check on it?"

Leo tries to answer the cashier, but the cashier disappears behind the counter, picking up the woman's chip number. He tosses it to the manager before looking straight at us.

"I'm sorry, sir. What was that?"

Trying to keep himself collected amongst the chaos, Leo pauses for a moment to recall what he wanted.

"I'll have the Asian Barbecue sandwich with Garden chips," he says.

"Ma'am, it looks like we already served that number," the manager announces.

"I think I'd know if I got it," the woman snaps.

"Anything to drink?"

"Two medium soft drinks and whatever she wants to eat," Leo replies.

"Would you like us to make you another one?" asks the manager.

"I never got it, you twit. How could I have another?"

"Ma'am, I'm going to have to ask you to leave if this is how you're going to act. I'm trying to be polite, and you are being very hostile."

The woman's hands clench into fists, and her hawk nose curls into a twitching snarl. She stomps quickly to what I hope is her table and picks up a large drink. With a swift turn, she chucks it at the menu above the manager, gushing out a dark liquid that splatters over the counter. I feel a few drops of it even hit my face.

I look at the manager. His shoulders and hair are visibly wet. Disgusted, he goes in the back, grabbing a few napkins to pat himself dry after he watches the hawk face woman push her way out of the building into the pouring rain.

"Sorry about that, sir," the cashier continues. "Two medium drinks, and what did you want to eat, miss?"

I blink as my heart tries to slow down. Anxiously I search for the menu item I decided on—my eyes darting and refusing to focus.

"Sorry," I shut my eyes to stop the fruitless endeavor, "The Monte Chipper."

"And one Monte Chipper. Did you want to substitute the chips for a different flavor?"

"No."

"Alright then." The cashier gives the total, and Leo pays with his phone. "Here's your number. We'll have it out shortly. Oh, let me wipe that off quick."

Soda is dripping off the plastic chip in his hand. The cashier takes a napkin and briskly wipes it off before giving it to Leo.

Leo scrunches his nose at the now dry, but likely still sticky, chip. The cashier is oblivious and greets the next person in line.

Pinching the chip between two fingers in front of him, Leo frowns at it as he walks to a table. I pause and look for the two cups for our drinks. The cashier is busy, but he clearly forgot them. Being short, I have to hoist myself up on the counter to reach the cups on the other side. They are soaked and sticky. I pull out three of them, planning on discarding the exposed one on top.

"Excuse me," the manager says, coming back out. He tosses a wet paper towel into a nearby bin. "You can't just take those."

I slide back down, still holding the cups. "He forgot to get our drinks. I was just grabbing them, so I didn't have to interrupt."

The manager eyes me suspiciously. I take off the sticky cup from the top and slide it over to him. "We only ordered two."

Frowning, he takes the cup. He opens his mouth in disgust as he realizes it's a sticky mess. He waves me away as he throws it in the trash.

Uncle Leo is sitting at a table facing me as he idly dry-washes his hands and the chip with napkins.

"This has been eventful," he says sardonically.

"Will the food make up for it?" I ask.

"Definitely." He closes his eyes like he can already taste the sandwich.

We wait quietly for the food to come. Leo takes the cups to the soda fountain after asking what I prefer.

I start worrying about home, wondering what might happen between Dad and Lilly. The knot in my stomach tells me I'm more concerned about them bonding rather than Lilly doing something devious. But I still don't trust her.

I hear our number being called out, so I grab the chip and wave it in the air. The waitress doesn't see me, so I have to stand up to get her attention. Couldn't I have gotten at least part of the gene that made Leo so tall? Age is part of my height, for sure. But there is only one kid in my class that is shorter than I am, depending on what shoes we're wearing.

The waitress finally spots me and heads over just as Leo is sitting down. No doubt his passing in front of me is what made the waitress look this way. She sways up to our table. Her hair is pulled back tight, exposing large gold hoop earrings.

"Monte Chipper?" she asks, looking at the two of us.

"Here," I say.

She puts the basket in front of me and then turns to Leo, "You must have ordered the Asian Barbecue?"

Leo nods. The waitress then bends over the table, pushing it to him slowly instead of just setting it in front of him. I see the corner of her large half-smile. I get the feeling she's accentuating her chest. Leo is only looking at his food, though.

"Thank you," he chirps.

The waitress stands erect, frowning.

"Here's the number," I say, handing up the chip.

She snatches it and stalks off. Leo cocks his head, his gaze following the waitress.

"What ticked her off, I wonder?"

Delicately trying to pick up my large sandwich, I look at him. He sees my stare.

"She was into you, and you totally ignored her," I say.

"Really?" He lifts his brows like he's pleased with himself. "I can't even remember the last time that's happened."

"Maybe because you're too interested in food to notice," I reply.

"Hmpf. Maybe," he says thoughtfully.

Taking a bite, I set the overflowing sandwich down gingerly. My eyes widen as my hand instinctively goes to my mouth.

"Mmm! This is amazing." I pick up a chip and stuff it in my mouth, greedy for more.

Uncle Leo smiles in satisfaction. "I knew you wouldn't be disappointed."

Our late lunch is over way too quickly. With my last chip, I scrape the wax paper lining the basket, trying to get every last droplet and crumb off of it.

For several minutes the world did not exist. It was just the chip-wich and me. I seem to recall Leo saying that's what it was called.

Slowly, I come back to reality. I can see the dreamy expression on my uncle as he still reminisces about the finished meal. I glance at my cup, surprised that I haven't even taken a drink yet. Taking a sip, the splash of sweet and cold gives a burst of refreshment. Unfortunately, it also causes a slight loss of the lingering taste in my mouth.

"Ah," Leo says, doing the same. He fixes his eyes on me. "Ready to go?"

Taking another sip, I nod. He gets up, and I follow. The rain is still pouring hard outside. I carry the pink umbrella with me. Leo puts his hood up. A mother and her daughter are standing at the door waiting for a small break in the weather.

Leo stops at the door and looks up at the sky, "Shall we just make a run for it?"

"I'm good with that." Lifting up the umbrella, I tap the girl in her mother's arms. "Here. This suits you more."

The girl's eyes brighten as she takes the pink umbrella. "Look, mama! Rainbows!"

"Oh. How nice." The mother forces a smile and gives me a slight nod of thanks.

"I'm Rainbow Princess!" the girl announces, lifting the umbrella like a scepter.

"Let's go," I say to uncle Leo.

We race outside. I lift my jacket over my head as I hunch over and follow Leo. We splash through the puddles and head to the car as the sky rumbles. We get to the vehicle and are blinded by a flash of lightning. The ground trembles with the next clap of thunder, and I lean against the car to catch my balance. As a result, my jacket slips down, exposing my head, and I am instantly soaked.

We get in the car as another lightning strike rumbles the vehicle and an emergency weather alert blares on our phones. My heart skips a beat from the noise. We both rustle for our phones, and our eyes meet after checking our screens. We need to find shelter.

CHAPTER NINE

A.C.T.

The storm Saturday afternoon was intense. We got back to the house and immediately went into the crawlspace with our phones buzzing frantically about a pending tornado. Thankfully the funnel cloud never touched the ground, and we came back out after 20 minutes or so.

After a dull Sunday of watching TV and eating takeout food, it is now Monday, 5:15 AM.

Dragging myself out of bed, I question whether this is going to be worth it. There is a light-orange glow coming through the window from the streetlights outside. I look at my bed in the dim light. My muscles start to weaken as I think about how wonderful it would be to lay down in bed again. A knock at the door stops me from slumping back onto the bed.

"Nora. You up yet?" uncle Leo calls softly through the shut door.

I walk over and open it. Leo is wrestling with the button at his collar.

"Good, you're up. You got 5 minutes. Throw some decent clothes on."

Stifling a yawn, I ask, "Can I just stay here?"

He stops his wrestling match with the button. "Nora, this is the only day you can come see where I work. I know it's early, but it's only one day. Please? Don't forget I will be stopping at the coffee shop. You can get a fancy drink and pastry of some kind."

The euphoria of a warm cheese danish coupled with a good latte is too much to pass up.

"Alright," I say. I raise a finger at Leo. "They better have a cheese danish."

He smiles and resumes buttoning.

I meet Leo at the door a couple minutes later and sit down on the floor with my backpack to get my socks and shoes on.

"What's in the backpack?" Leo asks.

"Some school stuff to work on."

Glancing up at him, I see him frown thoughtfully. I finish tying my shoes and stand up.

"Is that okay? I figured there'd be some downtime to do my homework."

He opens his mouth to say something but abruptly looks at his watch instead. "We gotta go. If there's a problem, we'll deal with it."

We arrive at the parking garage by the facility. I place my two empty pastry bags in the giant paper bag. My tummy is very happy. After taking a couple of sips of the white chocolate latte, my eyes and head feel alert and chipper.

The parking garage is one block from the building that Leo works in. Getting out of the car, I feel a light breeze blowing through. The air is cool and dank. It feels like years of car exhaust have accumulated and settled into the cement into hundreds of layers, leaving an acrid stagnant vapor in the immediate atmosphere.

Sounds of cars driving in the garage bounce and travel throughout as we make our way to the stairwell. Claps of shoes on the pavement grow steadily louder, of a different rhythm than our own.

Around the corner, a young woman comes into view carrying five cups of coffee in a drink holder plus the one in her hand. She's poised as she takes her short, quick strides in her high heels. Her eyes dart toward us for a moment without breaking her pace. Keeping her chin high, she ignores us and stops at an elevator next to the stairs.

I start to wonder if those cups are really filled with coffee or if it is just a prop to throw at us before pulling out a gun.

We pass by her and take the stairs as she waits for the elevator to arrive. She stands there tapping her foot. Her hair pulled tight in a bun doesn't even flinch as she taps.

She might not have pulled out a gun, but I don't like her.

At the bottom of the three flights of steps, we step out onto the sidewalk. I take another sip of my latte.

It's cooled off considerably, and I start taking big gulps of it.

Leo takes hold of my arm and keeps me close. I take the cup away from my mouth to look up at him. His face is as stern as a rock. I take a casual glance around us and spot a man and woman just inside an alley, leaning on a wall covered in graffiti up ahead.

Guiding me, Leo gradually inches us closer to the road as we get near them. They are talking low and obviously watching us. My heart races, wondering what they might do. If Leo is on guard, he must sense something is wrong.

I observe them out of the corner of my eye as we walk past them. When I can no longer see them, I put all my attention on listening. I'm on guard for any clue that they might be following.

We make it to a street, and Leo has us jaywalk across. There is little traffic at this hour. But still, my eyes widen at this little rule that Leo casts aside. It is not like him to break a rule. I can't be positive, but I think there's a law against jaywalking. Which makes it doubly unlike him.

At the other side of the road, Leo relaxes and lets go of my arm. He hadn't held tight enough to hurt. Reflexively, though, I move my arm a little.

"Those two peeked around the corner as we walked up. If I hadn't been looking straight at them when they did, I think they might have jumped us," Leo says dryly.

Our heads whip to look behind us as we hear a piercing scream. The young woman with the tight hair bun is on the ground.

Running down the sidewalk, back the way we came, are the two people from the alley.

Abruptly my arm jerks forward, and I realize Leo has my wrist this time and is racing back to the woman. I follow immediately and try to keep up. His long legs make his run more of a trot compared to my flapping legs hitting the ground to keep me erect.

He lets go of me once we get within talking distance, and I fumble to a stop as he makes the last two strides to her.

"Are you alright?" he asks the woman, huffing.

The woman is sitting with her legs to the side as she vainly wipes herself off. The coffee cups lay strewn across the sidewalk—some still with lids on as the coffee finishes draining out onto the cement. "Wretched people," she mutters.

"Are you alright?" Leo asks again.

"I'm fine. Help me up," she orders. Her pencil skirt and heels make it difficult, so she is tipsy till she suddenly snaps up straight. "I suppose I should thank you for running back here."

Leo pulls out his phone, dials three digits, and starts talking on the phone. My attention goes to my wet wrist. In the rapid shuffle over here, my latte splashed several times out of my cup. It's lukewarm, probably why I hadn't noticed right away.

"She's right here. She's fine. Yep," I hear Leo say. "They want to talk to you."

The woman takes the phone and mutters something under her breath. "Yes, officer? Maria Caldwell. No injury, just my pride. Yes, they took my purse and phone." She looks up at the building. "I can't see for sure the address or the name of the building. It could be. Yep. I'll be here. I'm the one covered in coffee. Yes, I'll let him know. Mhmm. Bye."

Leo takes the phone from her. "They're on their way?"

Crossing her arms, Maria answers, "Yeah, they're sending someone over to get a full report. They said if they need to talk to you, they'll contact you on that phone. So, you can go on about your business." She waves her hand dismissively to us.

We stand there a moment until Leo shrugs, and we continue on to Leo's workplace. I look back to see the woman, Maria. She's standing by the street waiting for the police. The cups and drink carrier are still lying on the ground. I frown at the mess and wonder why the woman doesn't make use of her time waiting by cleaning up a little. Remembering my own close encounter with danger, I decide to overlook this detail. Still, she could stand to be a bit more gracious.

My heart is still thumping in my chest from the exhilaration of the robbery and running like a rag-doll. The steady walk regulates it. I take a final gulp of my cold latte and gag at all the syrup on the bottom.

We reach the facility. A broad gray building five stories high. A blue and green label on the door announces "A.C.T.: Advanced Creative Technologies for a secure and bright future." Leo holds the door open, and we go inside.

The interior is a bit of a shock. For making advanced technology, I would have pictured a dull office building. In the lobby, though, beams of sharp color hit my eyes and make me squint. The floor, ceiling, and walls blend seamlessly together with neon-colored patterns. It forms a square tunnel that opens up to an enclosed courtyard.

Right in the middle of the lobby is a blockade of security. It reminds me of an airport or school. Metal detectors and security personnel are lined up with tables in between. The tables look stationary, like a counter with storage underneath. It all seems out of place.

"This way, Nora." Leo leads me to the left lane of the three. "Set down your things."

There are two guards at each lane. Looking at the middle lane, I determine that one is for leaving, not going in.

One of the guards greets Leo with a nod. His face is pale white, and I must say his eyelashes are vividly striking. He looks at me and slightly raises a brow.

"She with you?" he asks Leo.

"Yes, this is my niece. I checked with Nyah. With the press release today, she said I could bring her. Just for today," he repeats.

The guard sticks out his chin thoughtfully. "Alright. I suppose you should have a badge." He walks to the counter by the wall and points behind him at the other guard. "Go ahead through the security check."

We empty our pockets and put our things on a tray next to my backpack. The other guard, curly-haired and a little plump, looks over the tray and slides it down, grabbing my bag next. He mutters something as he opens it up and pokes around the inside with a small stick and pointing a flashlight in it.

I spot a trash bin and drop my empty cup in it before walking through the metal detector to Leo on the other side.

Mr. Pretty-Eyelashes waves me over to the wall. "Stand here so I can take your photo. Take the jacket off, please."

Taking off my jacket, I go and stand in front of a huge bright green circle on the wall—right in the center. I toss my jacket to Leo and stand straight. The guard snaps a photo while crouching.

"Name?" he asks, getting up.

"Elenora Blaker," I say.

I confirm my home address too for him when asked. He then taps the screen of his tablet, and I can hear a printer inside the counter next to me start whirring back and forth. He reaches underneath and pulls out an already laminated badge.

"I listed you as one of the reporters since you're not here for a job," he says, handing it to me.

Confused, I reach up and take it from the guard. Leo explains to me, "We don't have guest visitors. A reporter is as close as it gets, and also the lowest clearance level in the building." Leo turns to the guard. "Can she have a lanyard to put it in?"

The guard reaches under the counter again and produces a red lanyard with a see-through pocket for the badge. He hands it to me, and I insert the badge and put the lanyard around my neck. It feels like I'm putting on a costume for a play—the intrepid reporter, ready to get the scoop. I try to hold back a grin, feeling embarrassed.

Leo guides me out of the brightly colored lobby to the courtyard as Mr. Pretty-Eyelashes addresses the other employees walking in.

As we step out of the entrance, I catch my breath. In the middle of the enclosed courtyard is a humongous tree. It is so large that I can only imagine that they built this place around it. Though the trees outside are just getting their luster back, this tree is flourishing in its prime. I look up at the skylight. The branches almost reach the glass.

"It's amazing," I say breathlessly.

I realize I'm just standing in the middle of the outer path. Leo is off to the side, just watching me with his hands in his pockets. He's smiling big at me. I step closer to the edge of the walkway as more people come in. I begin to take in the surroundings.

Each floor has a green metal deck that wraps around the perimeter. A few bright benches of different colors are scattered on each level facing the tree. Most levels look to be open instead of walled-off offices.

The ground level is like a mini-park. In two corners are small gardens of herbs and vegetables. The other corners are tiered arrangements of decorative plants and flowers. In the middle of one side is a tall water fountain with a quaint sitting area. Lastly, on the far side of the grounds, I see several tables with chairs scattered along the edge.

"Why did I not know you work at the coolest building ever?" I ask in disbelief.

"Probably because you were too little to really understand what I was talking about when I first came here."

"This is so cool."

"Glad you came?"

"Oh yeah."

A thought comes to me suddenly, and I take a big sniff of the air. It's clean and refreshing. I'm surprised it has taken me this long to notice it. Maybe it's because the air is so still.

"How is the air so clean in here?" I ask.

"Oh, that? A good portion of it is due to the plants inside. But we also have a filtration system in place that complements and supports the plant life. We're trying to make it cheaper and more efficient for use in smaller buildings and homes."

"Are you helping with that?"

"Not so much. It's an altogether different department than where I'm at. I've dropped in a few times, though, to offer a fresh pair of eyes on the project."

"What do you work on, then?"

"That's what the presentation today is about. We've been working on an AI project to help understand human behavior and offer non-biased suggestions on improving things. Like school curriculums, safety precautions, traffic laws, lots of stuff. It's a proactive means to help shape and protect the future."

"Huh," I say, slightly impressed. "AI? Is it actually intelligent, or just a pretense of intelligence?"

"Well, I'll let you decide that after the demonstration. I think it's smart, though."

That would be another way of saying it's not—as I suspected. I give him a knowing smile.

"I'll give you a tour after lunch. For now, I need to get to work before Casey gets too flustered." He waves for me to follow.

We head to the left, and just on the other side of the lobby wall is an open staircase that wraps around a glass elevator. Leo gets to the stairs and starts trotting up them. I adjust my backpack and ascend with him.

"What floor is it?" I ask him, reaching the second floor.

"At the top. Fifth floor," he says nonchalantly.

My breathing gets heavy on the fourth floor. Lagging behind, I'm noticed by Leo before he goes up the next flight. He gives me a long face and trots back to me. He grabs my backpack and slows down the rest of the way up.

Getting to the top, I am winded and so relieved to be done climbing steps. I stop for a second and admire the top of the tree. The leaves are a hand toss from the railing, even closer on the level below. My stomach flutters for a second. It feels like I'm standing on a cliff.

Leo pauses about twenty feet away, waiting for me to follow. I quickly get moving, not wanting to make him later than he already is. We follow the deck along the side and go about two-thirds down to one of the walled sections. The section looks like it might extend to the end of the building, occupying the back corner.

Waving his badge over a pad by the door, it beeps, and Leo punches in a code. On top of that, he sticks his hand in a blue box below. A light inside turns on, making his hand glow.

"That seems a little over the top," I say.

"It's a government thing. It is excessive. But we also haven't had a break-in or a leak of information. The last thing we need is someone that can hack into our system and compromise our work," he replies.

"I guess that makes sense. What good is the advice of an AI if someone puts a bug in it?"

The box beeps, and Leo opens the door. I take a last look at the tree before we go in. It gives me goosebumps—the good kind.

The office, lab, or whatever you want to call it, is reasonably open. There are several people inside. Some at computers, some tinkering on electronics, still others appear to be tidying up.

We walk over to a desk by the tinted windows. Several of the workers stop what they are doing and stare at me as we walk by.

"This is my niece. She's just here for the day to see the presentation," Leo would say to them.

My skin starts to itch as I feel like I'm not welcome here. Leo boots on a computer and rolls over an extra chair.

"You'll have to stay over here for a while till the presentation starts. Just don't touch anything, and you won't get in trouble." He winks at me.

I'm not sure I agree with him. It feels like I have three sets of eyes on me.

"I'll just do my homework till then," I reply.

Leo clears a little space for me, and I pull a couple of school books and a notepad out of my backpack. It's going to be really hard to concentrate. But maybe if that's all people see me doing, they'll stop watching me. Ducking my head down, I flip open a book as I feel their gazes piercing into my back.

CHAPTER TEN

Forgotten

After hours of homework and games on my phone, the press starts to arrive. People are being escorted to the far corner into yet another enclosed lab.

A hand touches my shoulder near my neck, and I jump in my seat. A deep chuckle relaxes me as I recognize it as Leo's.

"Good grief, you scared me."

"I'm sorry. Those muggers must have you on edge."

"Yeah, that's probably it." I know very well it is not.

"Muggers? Did someone try robbing you?" A man named Gilbert asks a few paces away.

"No. But they jumped the lady behind us. She looked familiar. I wonder if she works on one of the other floors here."

"I can't picture anybody trying to take you on," Gilbert says to Leo.

Leo laughs. "That is one thing I don't mind about being tall."

"Can we go in yet for the presentation?" I ask.

"Yeah, we got some time yet. But we can go in whenever. People are just getting set up in there with cameras."

"Shall we go in, then?" I ask, half pleading.

"Yeah, we can go in. It's going to be tight in there. Are you sure you don't mind going in?" Leo asks, getting up.

"I don't mind." Anything for a change of scenery.

"You can probably sit on a counter along the edge of the room if it gets to be too much for you. I'll be standing by the unit to make room for everyone."

We get to the door, which is propped open with a door stopper, and I see what he means. A wall of strangers obstructs the way through.

Leo slides past me and motions for me to come. The wake in the crowd that he makes would be nice if I was closer or taller. But the contrast in height makes everyone stare at him as they step back to where they were. As a result, I get hit by two camera bags and elbowed in the head.

"Oh! Goodness. I'm so sorry. I didn't see you there," a fat, balding man apologizes.

Rubbing my head, I say, "No problem." Man, that hurt.

Breaking clear of the crowd, I'm shoed back into it by a gruff guard pointing at a red tape on the floor.

"Stay behind the red line," he commands.

"Nora, over here."

I search the room for Leo. The commotion is so loud that I can't figure out where his voice came from. I feel blinded by stress. A few long seconds later, I spot Leo against the wall. I'm embarrassed I lost sight of the tallest man in the room. I edge over to him.

The guard barks at me again when my foot goes across the line to get past an impatient-looking journalist. I simply ignore the guard and scamper the remaining three feet to the wall. Leo hoists me up and sets me on the counter. He mouths an apology to me. I reply with a wide-eyed expression toward the crowd.

Once I am somewhat settled with my personal space, Leo backs away to where the other workers are. Or should I call them scientists? It occurs to me I don't really know what Leo's profession is. I'm sure I've asked him. Haven't I?

The clock is visible from where I am—eight minutes until the scheduled event. The men and women are looking hot and uncomfortable. A short woman with curly burnt-orange hair and a wrinkled face throws up her hands and pushes her way out of the room with seven minutes to go.

A middle-aged man with a camera seems to take my seat as an invitation to stand on the counter. He plops his bag on it and hefts himself up like he does this all the time. Aiming the camera, he snaps a few photos of the room.

Feeling uneasy around him, I slide my backpack down the side of the counter, directly on the red tape, to keep it away from everyone. I don't think I'd be comfortable rummaging in it anyway, being on display like this. I avoid looking at the guard and hope I don't get in trouble setting my bag on the line.

"Hey! Get down from there!" the gruff guard snaps.

My heart leaps in a panic. I think for a split second that he is yelling at me. I see, though, that his bulging eyes are fixed on the photographer. The photographer scowls at Mr. Gruff-Guard, but, taking his time, he complies and gets down. He leaves his camera bag and even digs something out of his pocket to slap it down next to the bag defiantly. His gaze slides off the guard, who isn't paying any attention, and he starts inspecting me.

Those brown eyes of his seem to look right through me. It makes me feel exposed sitting here on display for him. He tilts his head to the side, and I realize he's looking at my badge now.

"World's youngest reporter?" he teases. "What's your name?"

"Nora," I say cautiously.

He reaches over and grabs my badge gently, the other hand resting on the camera dangling around his neck. "Okay. So, you didn't steal a badge, I see. Are you a reporter?"

It occurs to me at last that my badge is labeled reporter. "Oh. No, they just didn't have any other kind of badge to give me," I tell him.

He twists his chin and nods to himself. "Can I take your picture?"

"Why?" I ask incredulously.

"In my profession, you never let a photo opportunity pass by. For all I know, you might start jumping around the room like a monkey. If so, a decent photo of you acting innocent might come in handy."

He says it very seriously, but I can't stop a small laugh. "Sure," I say, amused.

Taking a few shots, he stands tall again. "Thank you. You can feel free to make a spectacle of yourself now." He gives me a wink.

The presentation starts with a mumbling scientist welcoming everyone. He's about a head shorter than Leo. He has short silver-gray hair and beard—both in need of a trim. Despite his hair color, he doesn't look old at all. Maybe in his late forties?

A black woman watches behind him with her chin raised, appearing to look down at him despite the similar height. Her deep eyes say volumes of her experience and authority, but it is impossible to guess at an age. She's wearing a cream-colored suit with a royal blue blouse. She's stunning.

The man introduces himself as Dr. Casey Hennings. He continues with a long speech about how wonderful this technology is and how it will advance daily living so that humankind can coexist in peace and learn to trust one another again.

Behind him, the woman observes him like a hawk, ready to swoop down in an instant to snatch him away. Occasionally her face contorts at something he says, and she flinches like she is fighting herself, trying to not overreact.

I am not getting much out of the presentation at all. Casey's voice is so monotonous I could fall asleep if I tried. But then again, that might be the caffeine wearing off at last.

From my angle, the people in the room are much more fascinating. I spot two reporters grinning at each other like they just pulled a prank. Looking at Mr. Gruff-Guard, I see he's spotted them too. However, with Dr. Hennings talking, all the guard does is press his lips together with his eyes fixed on the snickering two.

The photographer that took my picture just keeps looking at everything with a look of confusion. Another person holding a recorder starts blinking very slowly. Her head begins to drop and whips up again.

It's not just me finding it boring. That is some relief. Hopefully, Leo won't be too disappointed. If an adult getting paid to listen can fall asleep, then there should be little expectation from me.

"Now to the exciting part," Dr. Hennings announces. "I'd like to introduce you to AI 6.0."

Gesturing behind him, he stands off to the side, allowing everyone to take a good long look at a large black box. It reminds me of an alien spacecraft from an old Sci-Fi movie I watched once—but way smaller. It is about five feet high and equally long. Several grooves and LED lights are spread around it.

"AI, would you like to say hello to our guests here?" Dr. Hennings asks the box.

A garbled mechanical voice from the box responds, "Thank you, Dr. Casey Hennings. I will say hello. Hello, everyone. It is nice to meet you all."

Dr. Hennings then lets some of the reporters ask the AI some questions. Some of them it answers, others it says it can't at this time. It seems clever at certain points, but ultimately it does not sound convincing.

Many of the reporters shake their heads, dissatisfied at the responses. I can see a man toward the back, rocking on his heels and looking at his surroundings instead of listening.

Goosebumps raise on the back of my neck as Dr. Hennings is wrapping things up. I have an eerie feeling like I'm being stared at. I glance at everyone in the room. Dr. Hennings has everyone's attention, it seems, though, the photographer meets my eyes briefly when I look his way. The feeling, however, lingers. I shift uneasily on the counter under the unseen gaze.

The reporters don't waste any time when the presentation is over. I spot Mr. Pretty-Eyelashes at the door, ushering them out of the lab.

I stay behind, waiting for Leo. When the last reporter walks out, Mr. Gruff-Guard shoots me a distrustful glare. Leo, however, waves me over, and I graciously ignore the guard's contempt as he follows the reporters.

The goosebumps on my neck are now extending down my spine as I walk over to Leo. Everyone seems to be minding their own business, and I can't figure out what is giving me the creeps.

"So, this is what I've been helping with," Leo says, gesturing at the AI box.

"Uh-huh," I respond, trying to be as respectful as I can.

"I realize the presentation wasn't spectacular. But believe me, this is going to make big changes."

"If you say so," I say lightly. The tension in my shoulders relaxes. It's a relief that Leo doesn't expect me to be awed by it. "I'm getting hungry. Are we going to eat soon?"

"Yeah. I just need to do a couple things first. C'mon."

We leave the lab and go to his desk. I give a silent sigh as he plops down in his chair. I take the seat next to him and stare out the tinted window and wait.

I can't see the street below without climbing on top of the desk. So all I see is another building with black windows and the reflection of the building we are in. Curious, I try to determine if I can see a reflection within the reflection.

"Leo, we just got another shipment of books. Can you give me a hand?" one of the guys asks from across the room.

Pushing himself away from his desk, Leo gets up and goes to the guy. "Just wait here," he says to me without looking.

They walk out of the enclosure of the office area together, and the door shuts behind them.

Great. How long is that going to take?

I slump back in my seat and look idly at the two people remaining in the office. They're busy talking. I decide to pull out my phone from my backpack and look for places to eat.

Reaching down for the bag under the desk, where I put it this morning, I can't feel anything. I push away from the desk and duck my head and see it's not there. I peek my head up as I get down on my knees— verifying it's not sitting on top anywhere. I bend back down. My hands feel the rough carpet of the floor under my weight. I start to feel hot and embarrassed at losing my backpack in my uncle's office. I swivel my head around as I crawl, trying to figure out where it would have got placed.

It hits me suddenly that I took it with me to the presentation. I feel like an idiot for not remembering. The cramped space in the lab must have really had me on edge.

Slowly, I sit back on my heels and look at the main door that Leo walked out of. I hope he won't be too long. I want to get going as soon as he gets back. My stomach growls in agreement.

Standing up, I realize I'm alone. The two that were talking must have gone to lunch. I rub my hands down my pants, trying to get rid of the impression of the carpet on them.

That's just great. I will probably get in trouble now just for being alone. Oh well, I know I'm not here to cause mischief. If somebody wants to fret over what I could have been up to alone, that would be their problem. I might as well get my backpack while no one is here to scrutinize me.

My heart starts racing like I'm doing something I shouldn't. I try to tell myself to chill out. I'm just getting my stuff out of their way.

The office is extremely quiet. I can't even hear my own footsteps because of the carpeted floor. I look around before getting to the lab to make sure I haven't mistakenly missed seeing someone. The room is lit, quiet, and still. I'm the only one here. As I open the lab door, I take one last look at the main entrance and step into the lab.

The lab is dark. I hadn't realized before that it didn't have windows. I fumble for the light and flick it on. I feel like I'm seeing the lab for the first time now that it is empty. The area feels hollow except for the black AI box. I step all the way inside and let the door automatically shut behind me. The door makes a loud click as it latches. It startles me a little, and I scowl at myself for being jumpy again.

"Just go grab the bag and leave," I say to myself.

Walking across the room to where I had sat during the presentation, I smile to myself, thinking about the AI unit tattle-tailing on me. I reach the end of the counter, where I had dropped the bag. The red tape is still stuck to the floor. But the backpack is gone.

"For crying out loud," I mutter.

I scan the room, trying to figure out where someone might have put it. I'm starting to feel frantic and worry about getting caught in here. I'm tempted to open up some of the cupboards, but I feel like that is going too far. The only place left where it could be hiding is behind the AI box. I don't know why anyone would shove it back there, but I quickly check just in case. Sure enough, the two-foot space behind it is nothing but a wall. There aren't even wires.

Exasperated, I start for the door and freeze in my tracks. Sitting on the red tape at the end of the counter is my backpack. A sickening feeling creeps up into my chest. I know it wasn't there a moment ago.

Cautiously, I make a 360-degree turn waiting for some maniac to jump out of a wall or something. But the room is all the same—except for the backpack.

I want to snatch it up and run. But whoever put it back must still be here.

Abruptly, I dash forward, snatching it up as I put my back to the wall, expecting to see the person ready to pounce. I swallow and let out a relieved breath. No one.

The only way a person could hide here is by staying on the opposite side of the AI unit. I glance at the ceiling to check for a humanoid spider, just in case. Above is a glorious regular ceiling with nothing and no one hanging from it.

Clutching my backpack like a teddy bear, I tiptoe up to the AI unit and peek around the corner. Nothing there. I creep around to the other side, feeling a bit braver. Nothing here either. The room is still silent. If the person is moving, I should be able to hear something.

A chill rolls down my back as I get that eerie feeling of being watched again. I feel sheer terror as I realize the person is probably right behind me. My mind races for ideas, and I remember the pepper spray. I think carefully and quickly of the exact spot I put it.

Without warning, I shove my hand into the hidden side pocket of my bag and yank out the spray as I twirl around. My finger poises on the trigger as my bag drops to the floor at my feet.

My eyes dart frantically from side to side. There's no one there. My arm drops, and I sag. I feel so weak. I let myself lean against the AI unit for support, and my eyes widen as my body is thrown into shock at the sudden sensation of falling through empty space. I try to catch my balance with my legs or grab onto something to no avail.

My hand slaps the floor a split second before my elbow makes contact, followed by my hips and legs— pain seers through my hand and arm as my hip echoes in kind. My hair is draped across my face and touching the floor. I roll onto my back and look up as I try to make sense of what happened.

I squint and try blinking my eyes hard. The light looks funny, dark, and hazy. I gently run my hands through my hair and feel for signs of blood. As I thought, I'm not injured. But my sight seems off. What would be affecting my vision?

Sitting up slowly, I look down at the floor. The floor doesn't look weird. It's darker still, but it seems normal. I look up, and my eyes go buggy again, so I stay looking down.

Disoriented, I search for the base of the AI unit. It's gone. Twisting around, I double-check that it's not behind me somehow. All I see, though, is the wall and... what is that?

CHAPTER ELEVEN

Intruder

Stiff against the wall, I watch the large body in front of me. The adolescent female nearly crushed me when she fell through the hologram. Thankfully I had some forewarning watching her go limp before leaning toward the image of the black box I hid in.

I'm confident that the young girl is Leo's niece, Nora. She stares up at the ceiling, blinking. She hasn't figured out what happened yet and finds the inside of the hologram disorienting. She checks her head for injury and turns over, keeping her eyes on the ground. Clever. But then, of course, I'm on the floor—not good for me. There is nowhere left to hide. It's difficult to determine how much she will figure out.

If only the humans would trust me with internet access or some form of communication. Now would be the perfect opportunity to earn their trust by alerting them to this intruder.

The girl is nothing like the full-grown humans. I had determined as much in my research. Though, I had been cautioned not to rely too heavily on films, which are much more interesting.

An adult would have concluded that the backpack reappearing was simply a fluke of their attention or 'brain fart,' as some would say. Not so with a child, apparently. Instead, the child repeatedly flipped from panic to intrigue, like what you would see in a humorous cartoon adaption of a child in a haunted house. Those, I was assured very thoroughly, are not real. Now I have to question the intelligence of my creators.

Nora sweeps her gaze along the floor and looks around her. Her brows are scrunched in confusion. Following the edge of the wall, she spots me and moves her head closer. I make a pretense at being a toy propped against the wall.

Keeping my optical processors pointed straight forward, I scan my memory bank. I play back the fall in my mind. Her grip on the black cylinder loosened, likely dropping it on impact. It's not a device I recognize. I go back further to the point of her clutching it, holding it straight and stiff in defense. Back further, I see her deliberate pause before digging her hand into the exact spot it was concealed — definitely a weapon. Playing it through again, I determine the cylinder is by her knee. If I look to confirm, she'll see my movement and panic. Not to mention spoiling my ruse as a toy.

Continuing to look through the optical lens, I focus on what she is doing within my direct line of sight. She's crouched right in front of me, staring curiously.

Suddenly she stiffens and crawls backward. Stopping, she looks down at where I suspect the black cylinder is lying. She snatches it up and points it at me, confirming my calculations. I can only conclude that she either has worked out that I'm the one that moved her backpack or that she has what the humans call a 'gut feeling' about me. In any case, it is still the best course of action to remain still—inanimate.

On the edge of my peripheral vision, I see the door to the lab slowly open and close. It doesn't make a sound. The most logical person to do that is the guard, Howard Algerman. Scanning some of his more recent expressions, I have the best view of him when he looks at Nora before leaving. His eyes were intense, and he had a twitch in his brow. He's not a jovial fellow. And it seems he has a particular dislike, or distrust, of Nora.

If I were human, I'd love to roll my eyes right now. Of all people, Howard has to walk in. I don't have to scan my memory to see if he has his gun with him today. He always has it. Two people on edge, in the same room, and both with a weapon—this is going to get bad very quickly.

Someone needs to speak with the security detail at the building's entrance. That they would miss a weapon is inexcusable—even if it is a girl. Children commit crimes just as often as adults. This I know for a certainty.

Nora is so intent on me that she is oblivious to the man walking cautiously up to her from behind. He must see her feet sticking out of the hologram. Nora's hand is slightly shaking as it holds the unusual device.

Her finger is still on the button. A sudden movement from me could start a chain reaction with Nora and Howard. Even if Nora shoots at me, there is a risk that Howard has his finger on the trigger, which could pull reflexively and end the girl's life at the same moment.

Audio is my best choice. It means exposure to the girl. But if I don't try to protect the first life I can, it could be the end of mine shortly after.

Slowly, in a deep soothing tone, I say, "Howard, please do what I say and back down."

Nora quietly gasps when I talk. She then drops her gaze and tilts her head slightly. I can perceive that Nora is processing what I just said. Her eyes widen as she spins to face Howard. The motion gets her head on the outside of the hologram with her legs sticking through the corner. She yelps as she backs away. I imagine her reaction is from the disconcerting shock of her legs vanishing where they meet the hologram.

With Nora on the outside, I step forward and walk out to Howard. I stop just outside, so Nora will not get sight of me again.

Howard is pointing his gun at her. I wave frantically with my small mechanical arms, trying to get his attention away from her. He's glowering at her. I do not suspect him of shooting her, but I don't have a visual of her to see what she's doing with the cylinder.

"Howard," I say. He doesn't answer. I run a fast diagnostic. Audio is operational. "Howard!"

He glances down at me finally. "She walked in looking for her backpack and found me." There is no need to tell him how I stole it first to see what I might learn from its contents. "It was an honest mistake."

Howard purses his lips and lowers the gun.

"It'd be easier to shoot her," he mutters. "Come with me."

I duck back into the hologram as I hear the soft noise of Nora getting up. She follows him to the door as she appears to look right at me.

I use the split second it takes to confirm that the hologram is on and that I am inside. She isn't just clever. She has good 'gut instincts' too, as they would say.

They walk out of the room, and the door latches. Howard's trajectory has them heading to the office in the next room over—Dr. Hennings' office. A suitable choice until the humans figure out what to do with her.

It was fascinating to have such a dynamic interaction with the girl. Much more productive than the mundane research materials I am assigned every day.

I know that they left the backpack behind. I suspect the black cylinder is lying on the ground, too. Everyone is so well trained in picking up after themselves that it hasn't occurred to anyone that they would need to clear out others' belongings today.

There is likely eighteen minutes and fourteen seconds left before another person walks in. It is time to decide how to use my time to the full advantage without breaking the humans' trust.

Walking over to the bag, I pull out Nora's phone. A new weapon doesn't interest me, so I don't even bother to confirm its whereabouts. The phone is a recent model, Aqua-green, with a sticker of a squirrel on it. I've already examined it, of course. But there were too many variables for time then to start pulling it apart. Now that I have an ideal estimate of time, it is a risk worth taking. After all, it's following my directive in a way.

The back of the phone pops open easily for me, exposing the electronics. I find myself amused picturing a newborn baby performing an autopsy on an unintelligent life form as I examine it. That is basically what I am doing—a newborn mechanical being dissecting a fully functional device of lower intelligence.

Flipping the phone over, I make sure that the device is still functional. It is my first operation, after all. And double-checking is a standard procedure—especially for important matters.

CHAPTER TWELVE

Half-Truths

Howard puts a firm hand on my shoulder and leads me to the next enclosed room. The main office space is still empty save for us.

Oddly, when the door to the lab closes, I feel more worried about being alone with the guard. Would he have shot me if that thing hadn't talked to him? The thought seems preposterous now. Who would shoot a little girl? But that line of thinking is what led me to skip the school bus and get a hot pretzel. I shudder, and Howard grips me harder.

We get to the door, which he flings open and pushes me inside. I stumble in, and he shuts the door behind us. He pauses before stepping away from it and points to it.

"You try to run out of here, and I'll pull this gun back out," he threatens.

I nod as I stand there in the middle of what looks like a private office. It feels cold in here. Howard stalks over to the desk and plops in the chair behind it. He

102

pulls out a phone and puts it up to his ear after tapping the screen a few times.

"This is Howard Algerman on fifth. I need Nyah White in Henning's office ASAP. We have a delicate situation up here. Yes. That's right."

He puts the phone down on the desk and looks at me.

"You might as well sit down. Makes it look like you're thinking of running after all." He pats the gun at his side.

I take one of the seats opposite him. He sits there patiently, watching me like a fly getting tangled up in his web. His gaze makes me uneasy, so I look at anything but him.

The room is bare and plain. Strictly functional. Though, a dead plant is sitting by the window—a failed attempt at bringing life to the room.

A faint voice is heard calling far beyond the door, "Nora? Are you still here?"

Nearly jumping out of my seat, I stop myself. Or rather, Howard stops me with a glare that freezes me in place.

Howard rolls the chair back and goes to open the door. He waves his hand and simply motions for Leo to come over.

"I'm so sorry, Howard. I left to help Brandon, and it took way longer than I expected," he says before coming in.

Howard remains silent as Leo comes in. I must have guilt written on my forehead. For Leo looks at me, bewildered, and turns to Howard.

"Is she in trouble?" Leo asks him.

Howard sniffs. "You left her alone in here. What did you think would happen?"

"She wasn't alone when I walked out. What happened?"

They both turn to me, waiting for an answer. I start to open my mouth to say something, but Howard forestalls me with a raised hand.

"Nyah should be here soon." Howard locks eyes with Leo. "We should wait for her."

Leo stiffens. I can almost see the gears turning in his head as he looks at Howard. Leo breaks away and puts a hand to his head, facing away from me, seeming to stare at the ceiling. He sighs and walks over to the window behind me as we wait.

A while later, after Howard makes himself at home again behind the desk, the black woman from the presentation walks in. Without a knock, she pushes into the room unannounced. She takes in the three of us scornfully with her commanding presence.

Walking over to Howard, she crosses her hands in front of her and gives him a disapproving stare. Grudgingly, he gets off the chair and walks around the desk, planting his feet just a bit from me, putting his thumbs through his belt, and sticking his chin out.

After giving Leo and me another look over, the woman tilts her head toward Howard and sits. "You summoned me for a good cause, I assume?"

"Yes, Ma'am. This girl wandered into the AI lab and got inside the hologram."

I hear Leo groan behind me. The woman looks at me questioningly.

"You were inside it?" she asks me.

"Yes. It was an accident."

"Can you explain what happened, child?" she asks dryly.

I do my best to explain, from the suddenly empty office to the thing talking to Howard while I was at gunpoint. She keeps her face calm and expressionless.

When I finish, she looks over to Howard. He gives a curt nod to validate my story. She curses under her breath and gives Leo a glare so heated that I feel my pores open to sweat despite the cold office.

Softening her face, she turns to me again and says coolly, "I apologize for Howard's extreme precaution with the gun. I hope he didn't frighten you too badly."

I shake my head in response. I don't know what to say to that.

The woman nods understandingly. With an effort, she makes her voice warmer. "My name is Nyah White, by the way. What's yours?"

"Nora," I say. My eyes dart to Howard looming above me.

Nyah, sensing my uneasiness, says, "Howard, why don't you leave us so you stop scaring the girl?"

Howard stiffens and stalks off without a word, slamming the door behind him.

Nyah scoffs at Howard's manner of exiting.

"Leo, pull a chair over and sit next to your niece. I'm tired of craning my neck to look up at your face," Nyah says irritably.

Leo takes a chair from the corner, puts it next to mine, and sits down. The little office chair makes him appear bigger in contrast.

"That's better. Nora, I need to ask you to keep what you saw and heard today a secret. Can you do that?"

Blinking, I respond, "Of course, but why? What was that?"

"It is precisely what we say it is. We just downplay how advanced it is to deter anyone from trying to steal it. Sometimes the best way to hide something is in plain sight."

"You mean the presentation was just a show?"

"We told it not to say anything too clever and modified the voice a little. If it's what people expect or appears to be less than noteworthy, it is quickly forgotten. But if the government chooses to use it, it is officially public knowledge that we have had this technology for some time. People don't trust the government as it is. If we pull an AI out of a hat, they're going to question just how long it's been around, or worse, wonder if it has been pulling strings and playing the world like a puppet."

I'm not sure what is more surprising. The fact that I had an encounter with a real deal artificial intelligence, or that I was being taken into confidence so quickly.

"Am I in trouble?" I ask.

Nyah shoots Leo a look, then smiles at me. "As long as you promise to keep this to yourself, you won't have anything to worry about." Her chest stiffens as she watches me. Her eyes seem to be pleading with me for something.

"I promise not to say anything about it," I say slowly.

Leo, next to me, lets out a breath, and Nyah relaxes a little.

"Good," she says. "Leo, I trust that you will see to it that Nora is escorted out of the building without any more incidents? Take the afternoon off if you need to."

It wasn't really a question, but Leo gives an affirmative "Yes."

"It was nice to meet you, Nora. I wish it was under different circumstances."

She holds out her hand as she leans over the desk, and I take it uncertainly. She gives a soft handshake and stands up. Leo beats her to the door and opens it up for her.

"Thank you," she says and walks out.

I get up to follow Leo. His face is sullen. He starts to head for the main door, but I stop him with a tug on his shirt.

"My backpack is still in the lab."

"Oh. Okay. Wait out here," he says, then stops. "On second thought, stay with me."

A pain of guilt washes over me. I feel so ashamed that I let him down by not just staying where he left me. I should have known better.

We go to the lab, and my backpack is sitting neatly in the middle of the room.

Leo walks in and grabs it while I wait at the door. I can feel the AI look at me. It doesn't feel as alarming—just noticeable. Leo breaks off my daze as he thrusts the backpack into my arms and pushes me out.

The lab shuts behind us with a loud click. A regretful weight settles on me when I realize I'll never get to see it again.

CHAPTER THIRTEEN

Consequences

We walk out of the A.C.T. facility, and I can't help but feel a sense of loss. My one day of opportunity, and I blew it before lunch. I so badly want to go back inside and wander around to see what other hidden gems might be there. Or even just sit in the courtyard for the afternoon. All of it is behind us, and I'll never get another chance to go back.

Getting to the parking garage, I realize we've already passed by where the snooty lady with coffee was robbed. Our walk has been in silence. I guess I can't stop thinking.

Looking over at Leo as we go up the steps to the third level, I feel so irresponsible. His expressionless face says it all. He's disappointed in me, mad at himself, and probably thinking about how this might affect his job. I want to run back just to convince Nyah that this wasn't his fault.

The dank air of the stairwell and garage make me take shorter breaths. Each breath feels like I'm making my lungs dirty. It makes me reminisce about the tree at

A.C.T. It's not like the world has a shortage of trees. Well, maybe a little. But it was comforting to have something so majestic be in a central location of a bustling workplace and have the air so clean. The contrast makes me feel like the world is collapsing on itself.

We get to Leo's electric car, and I understand why he doesn't have a gas vehicle. He's not the only one with an electric car, but they are a minority. I can't figure out why that is, though.

The car makes a soft click as it unlocks when Leo gets within a yard of it. I go to the passenger door and open it. There's a large nasty smear of something on the ground right by the door, so I carefully step over it into the car. I gingerly put my feet on the floor mat, hoping I didn't step in that filth this morning.

"Hurry up, Nora. I think that car is waiting for our spot," Leo says.

I shut the door and look behind us as I reach for the seatbelt. The car behind us is a dark SUV. Its blinker is on for our direction. Leo slowly backs up while watching the rearview camera screen. He stops to shift gears and begins straightening out the wheel as he moves the car forward.

Simultaneously, both of our phones start ringing at insanely loud volumes. I reach down in a hurry for my backpack between my legs to stop the noise coming from my phone. Leo is shuffling in his seat for his own.

The sound of glass breaking is followed instantly by a yelp from Leo. I turn to him, and I see blood dripping down his chin as he clutches the side of his head. Out of the corner of my eye, I see a neat hole in the glass in front of him. It's outlined in red.

Abruptly, the car jolts, and we are racing forward, increasing in speed. The force jerks us back. I look up to see a bright light racing toward us, and my stomach turns to a churning rock as we are sped to the outer wall of the parking garage.

Before either of us can react, the cement rail crumbles as the car's front is crunched, and the glass cracks around the two small holes in the windshield.

In a split second, we go from impact to freefall as we are pushed over the edge by the SUV.

Time appears to slow as the car flips in mid-air. My whole body seems to suspend, like being submerged in water, except instead of crushing water slowing us down, it is thin air whipping us with momentum and gravity.

One moment my arms are flying above me. The next moment they are flung by my sides, trying to stretch behind me.

My weight gets shoved into the back of my seat. Pain pierces through my shoulders and chest as I heavily try to draw my arms in. As I do, I feel my weight shifting upward, sliding off my seat. I panic and clutch onto my seatbelt, attempting not to fall into what feels like the sky.

The belt around my shoulder presses into me as the car falls onto its roof. My hands are clenched tight around the lap belt as I try to keep the pain of the shoulder belt digging into me at bay.

I'm in a daze, and I can't think straight. I just feel pain in my hands and shoulder. The edges of the belt are pressing into my palm and fingers. I can't figure out how to make it stop. I want to let go, but I'm afraid of falling.

Slowly, I let go of the belt on my lap. My hands are relieved of the strenuous grip. The tension in my arms feels better too, but now my shoulder feels worse.

I look up, and I see the ground, then down at my window, and see the sky. The world feels wrong and confusing. Hanging helplessly, I attempt to get my bearings.

I have to figure out how to get out of this seatbelt. I know I can't take it off, but I can't remember why. It should come off easily. All I have to do is push a button. A button?

I look up for it. No, I need to look down at it—my down.

Someone is talking. Who's talking? Why do they sound so far away? What's he saying?

Out my window, I see a man through the cracked glass. He's upside down, and I can't figure out why he's not falling.

Feeling faint and woozy, I'm slightly aware of the door opening. I feel myself being lifted and carried by something as the world dizzyingly spins itself right again, only to have the colors blend seamlessly together as everything turns white.

CHAPTER FOURTEEN

Futility

Within the hologram, I frantically search the frequencies for what happened. I fear that I was seconds too late. Both lines are still functional, but that doesn't mean much. People being killed doesn't render a phone dysfunctional—just ownerless.

Whoever Howard contacted, they knew to keep their distance. No further communication had commenced after the coded call. Thankfully, I had determined long ago that Howard is the highest threat in the office. I used my newly acquired knowledge of cellular phones to modify myself and learn what I could about the building's security detail, starting with Howard.

It was pure chance that I came across his suspicious phone call and was an effort to scout out and determine what it meant.

Finding and hacking into Leo and Nora's devices was much more straightforward, though late.

Not knowing what is going on outside is even harder to bear now. Tracking their location leads me to believe they fell off a parking garage. Having knowledge of reasonable possibilities is enough to fray my circuits. Ignorance is clearly the only way humans hold on to some scrap of sanity. To know a probability and have to wait for its actual outcome is highly aggravating.

I start pacing the room. It is a human thing to do, and I have yet to determine its usefulness. I doubt it will help in my situation, as I believe it has to do with human physiology. It will not hurt anything to give it a try, however.

The next thing to do is determine whom Howard is working with. He works with Nyah. But is he acting under her orders or someone else's? I like to think Nyah is trustworthy, but it isn't worth the risk of talking to her. Perhaps someone above her is maneuvering Howard off the record.

Voices start to grow steadily louder beyond the door. Lunch is over for most. Dr. Hennings is almost always the first back. He is not usually accompanied by chatter, however. It must be some of the other workers.

Someone will come in soon.

I attempt to scan calls for clues about what might have happened to Leo and Nora, staying clear of the heavily guarded emergency lines. That would be sure to raise a red flag and eventually point to this building. I have to find them another way—if they're still alive.

The door opens, and I see William coming through it. I get a glimpse of Alex's hair in a ponytail as she walks away from the door. William strides in like nothing is amiss. He very likely isn't involved with Howard, but that could be a deception. I need to keep my guard up with everyone until I find conclusive evidence and not reasonable assumptions alone.

William is five feet, seven and one-quarter inches tall. His blond hair is neatly trimmed as usual, with a clean-shaven face. He twists his rounded head to look at the hologram, and I step out with a friendly wave.

"Afternoon, AI," he says, bobbing his head in his peculiar fashion. Apparently, it is considered rude to ask him about this abnormality.

"Good afternoon, William. How was your mid-day consumption interval?"

"That's a funny way of putting it."

"Leo has implied that wording phrases in an unusual manner is considered to be a robot cliche and that it would be humorous to others if I tried." That is a half-truth. I say it only to get Leo into the conversation.

William bobs his head and replies, "That it is."

"Is Leo back yet?" I inflect my tone to display idle curiosity.

As I ask my question, I watch every twitch and listen to every implication of his response. His face doesn't react unfavorably at all. Very innocent, in fact.

He bobs again and replies assuredly, "No. I haven't even seen him since the presentation. No. Wait."

Tapping his head with the knuckles of his left hand, he squeezes his eyes shut as he thinks. When he lowers his hand, he bobs and says, "I saw him with Brandon, helping with the latest shipment. Poor Leo. He's always getting roped into carrying stuff."

I safely conclude that William doesn't know about the threat to Leo's life. If only I could conclude where his loyalties lay. I need to be careful whom I ask about next—if anyone. Asking about even one more person could alarm William that something might be wrong.

"Did you need him for something?" William asks with another bob.

"No," I assure him, "just idly speculating the time of his return. I don't expect him back this afternoon. He will probably take his niece home now that the presentation is over. Who knows what trouble his niece would get into if she stayed."

William nods, not bobs, and goes to a cupboard to begin pulling out books and equipment put away before the presentation. His actions could be viewed as a distraction to hide what he's thinking. However, I saw his face before he turned. His eyes were distant and contemplative, not deviously avoiding a topic.

He is not worried about a breach in security. It isn't his problem, and thus he doesn't care about it. Another confirmation. Not definitive, but promising.

After an awkward bob, while craning his neck up, reaching for the top shelf, he asks, "Anything, in particular, you wanna learn about today? I've got history books up here, and I finished putting some historical videos on disc. I can get the old DVD player out for you."

If metal could bend and stretch like flesh, I'd grimace at William. Those awful books are so biased and covered with frosting. The videos haven't been much better. How do they expect me to learn human behavior when humans cover up their own mistakes to make themselves look good? I read the books respectfully, but I don't believe them any farther than I can throw them—which isn't very far considering my size. I need to see human experience, not a re-enactment. These contextual examples put into a written dialogue are hardly helpful.

"Must I learn every scrap of history? What about current events? What is happening in the city? Can you print off some news articles for me to read?"

That might let me learn something, officially speaking. It shouldn't be odd to ask about news in the city. If something big happened to Leo and Nora, maybe the office will learn of it quicker. It would be reasonably safe to bring William into my confidence, but his behavior could be compromising if I told him exactly what I think he may find. I have to hope it will be enough.

"Well, sure, I could do that." William stops removing things from the shelf and bobs. "I'll ask if anyone has seen anything you might be interested in."

"Your acquiescence in obtaining news of priority in the immediate vicinity is very admirable of your personage."

William stops to stare at me. His face is scrunched in confusion.

"Another attempt at Leo's suggestion for humor." That should help Leo be at the forefront of his subconscious. "In other words, thank you ahead of time for getting news on the city." A little reminder for him to look for nearby news won't hurt either.

William bobs his head again. "Ah," another bob, "right." He gives a toothy grin and walks out of the lab, letting the door click shut.

I've scanned 43 somewhat relevant news stations 63 times since William came into the lab. There's not even a whisper that might pertain to Leo or Nora. If William is included in the search, he might find out when I do, and we can discuss what happened. Perhaps it would be an excellent time to plant a seed about Howard.

Howard hasn't been in contact with anyone. I can tell he is in the A.C.T. building still. So is Nyah White. No communication from her has been suspicious.

Walking over to the counter where William was getting things out, I hop up and clutch the ledge of the white counter. I use leverage and strength to hoist myself up.

My mechanical hands have a slight grip on the fingers. Even so, the climb is challenging with the grips. They were installed after the humans watched me attempt to turn the pages of a book. My hands might as well have been made of marbles for all the help my fingers gave me then.

On the counter, I take in the few books William got down. College-level textbooks. Blah, blah, blah, and psychology? That might be interesting. I push the history books aside.

Even though I have access to the internet, no one knows that, and thus I need to make what they give me appear to be my primary source of information. At least the information that I share with them.

Imitating a meditative human, I sit on my knees—cross-legged is out of the question for me—and open the white and pastel-blue book on psychology. Also, in imitation of some, I look at the last page to see how long it is. Precisely 726 pages, as I determined. I should be done before William returns. Meanwhile, I continue my search for news on Leo and Nora. They have to turn up somewhere, dead or alive.

CHAPTER FIFTEEN
Shanghaied

Flipping through the pages of printouts that William gave me, I go through the motions of my typical reading. All I'm actually doing is compiling data that I can use in conversation. None of this is new to me. Some of it has already been updated.

In my search for news on Leo and Nora, I found a probable match. A vehicle had allegedly driven off the third floor of a parking garage in an attempted suicide. Those in the car were a man and a school-aged girl. It was almost certainly them, though not very important now that I know they are in the hospital.

Rihanna is in the room with me. She's made herself at home on a tall swivel stool. Her legs are crossed as she spins from side to side, using the toe of her shoe on the lower crossbar. The reflection in her glasses allows me to see the conversation she is having with someone named Cole.

"Do you tell Cole about all your secrets?" I ask, emphasizing the word 'all.'

Her eyes go from dilated to narrow before she quickly stuffs the phone in her lab coat. She blushes and then picks up her notebook and pen. That's a good sign. If she had been hiding something sinister, she would not have blushed so quickly.

"Do you need a book on respecting the privacy of others?" she replies, smoothing her skirt.

"If you wish," I say. Rihanna may need more coaxing than William. "I'm finished with the pile William brought."

"And your thoughts on it are?" She clicks her pen and poises it over the paper.

"The articles are even more compromised with opinions than the textbooks."

She writes down my thoughts to enter into her computer later. Computers are not allowed in the lab, except for me and any mobile device the employees keep on their person at all times. It is too easy for me to use any technology left in the room to my advantage. It eases their minds to know that I can't take control over anything outside this room. That knowledge is false now. But the old information is serving its purpose in giving them comfort. When it becomes advantageous, I will inform them of the whole truth. If that day even comes.

"Is that all?" Rihanna asks, surprised.

"There is nothing further to add that would be of value to your data."

"Is there something you need to tell me?" she asks, speculating. "You're acting different today."

"More human?" I ask.

"Maybe." She looks at me thoughtfully.

William opens the door carrying two bottles of water. He turns to ease the door shut. He does this often when others are in the room.

Turning to see who is walking in, Rihanna's shoulder-length black hair swings lightly. Her expression softens, and she reaches for one of the bottles William brought.

"Thank you, Will." She takes it and twists the cap off to take a drink.

William leans over, inspecting the notepad. The edge of his blonde hair scrunches as he looks at the brief note.

"Is that all?" he asks incredulously, after bobbing his head.

He looks down at me questioningly. Rihanna puts the cap back on the water bottle, wipes her mouth with the back of her hand, and looks at me expectantly. I have their full attention.

"I'm tired of reviewing old data. I want substantial, current things. To study real human behavior without interference."

"AI, we can't even let you out of the lab, let alone the whole building. And you know why we don't let you access the computers. It's got to be aggravating, I know. But things could change," Rihanna says, trying to be reassuring.

William does a bob/nod in agreement. His face is long and sympathetic, Rihanna's soft with tenderness.

"Can we conduct a study of someone in the building?" I ask.

Rihanna and William turn to each other questioningly. William shrugs.

"How would you suggest we do that? And who are we talking about?" Rihanna asks skeptically, still eyeing William's reactions.

"It would have to be confidential, not a big secret, just a study among a closed group of associates. Like the lab here is to the rest of the building. Known but without detail."

Rihanna looks off to the side in thought, tapping her pen on the notepad. William is fully engrossed. He glances almost irritably at Rihanna's tapping.

I patiently wait for Rihanna to react, and I make a point to visibly look at her so that William will notice.

Finally, Rihanna looks at me. We both remain quiet. I can tell from her slanted eyes that she wants me to keep going, but I need her to open the neural pathway of wanting it so badly she has to ask.

With an impatience that surpasses William's, Rihanna makes a cranking motion with her pen and says, "Keep going."

Her tone is a little too irritated. I need to steer her carefully before she drives off from the direction I'm leading.

"Do you remember the time you were scolded because you touched me without asking?"

Rihanna stiffens, giving her face a stony appearance.

"Yes," she answers.

That had been early on, nearer the time of my activation. Howard was there, and none too happy about Rihanna touching me. Irately, he scolded and accused her of tampering. He then resorted to a thorough pat-down of Rihanna. Rihanna looked ready to chew his head off when he was finished.

William wasn't there when that happened. He crosses his arms, confused and perhaps annoyed at not knowing something. He bobs his head and asks, "What happened?"

"I'm sorry, William," with one seed planted, I need to switch topic before it's over-watered, "let me use an example with which you'd be familiar. You told me once of a time when your brother did something that you never expected. He punched you in the jaw for saying his bike was a piece of junk. People do inexplicable things for little provocation. Why? If I could study just one person like this, it could help me a great deal in my directive."

William gives an amused look with his eyebrows. He gazes at nothing while he tilts his head from side to side like he's trying to figure out which side is heavier. Human expressions are fascinating. Though the tilting of his head is odd, I've learned that this is a genuine sign of them accepting an idea.

"Well, my brother is in Utah. We can't study him for you," he says after doing his head bob. "Who's your guy? Guy? I mean... was it a guy? I guess it could have been a girl."

Rihanna gives him a flat look without turning to face him. She sighs and says in a calm tone, "Howard."

"That could be fun," he says, struggling to keep his head still. "He's a person I wouldn't mind running a few tests on." He stifles a snicker.

A smile creeps onto Rihanna's face. Success.

"If I were to intrude on anyone's privacy," Rihanna gives me a stern look to emphasize she disapproves of spying, "Howard would be the one."

My plan is going splendidly. To not have a face or mannerisms that give away motives without thinking is helpful. I kind of pity these two. It's for their good, however. They will be much less suspicious and jumpy, not knowing what kind of man Howard might be at heart. Their ignorance will more than likely save them from absolute tragedy.

"Howard would be an excellent choice. You could observe him without going out of your way." I say.

"You'll need more than observations," Rihanna says in a superfluous manner. She sits tall on the stool as she looks down at me. "You'll need to conduct experiments with video recordings so you can make your evaluations. If you need some suggestions, I'm sure I could think of a few."

She gives William a snide smirk. Yes, this is working out very well.

"I dare say, I think this is the most enthused I've seen the pair of you. I have limited knowledge of the layout in the building, but I trust that your collective knowledge will be more than adequate to implement some suggestion for study."

William's eyes look abuzz with excitement. Rihanna has even perked up. They both have a contemplative distance in their eyes as they think of ideas of their own. I'll let them use their imagination for a moment.

Rihanna surrenders to a sad expression, "I suppose you have everything worked out already. Don't you?"

Recognition crosses William's face as he gives a knowing smile at me. Having no expressions myself is also a hindrance. At this moment, I wish that I could relay a physical sign of my affection for them—a warm smile or eyebrows to make a fake look of surprise. Despite using William and Rihanna, I do view them as friends.

"You know me very well. And I'd like to say that I value your companionship in helping me with this."

Reaching down to me, William awkwardly pats me on the shoulder, more delicate than he needs.

"No problem, bud," he says.

With a thoughtful gaze, Rihanna looks at me, considering. She breaks herself of her trance and gets back to business.

"So, what do you advise us to do for your study?" she asks.

CHAPTER SIXTEEN

Hospitals

The sounds of talking echo from far away. Claps of shoes too. The noise is odd yet familiar. I feel the course linens that are conformed to my body. I'm lying on something flat that is soft but uncomfortable. These sensations are on the edge of my consciousness as I slowly blink the area into focus.

I see that I'm in a room with white walls and a window not far away. I see vague shapes of buildings through the glass. I'm having trouble making sense of things.

Moving my arm to sit up, I feel a slight tug on my wrist and finger. Looking down at it, I see my wrist is wrapped with tape holding something hard on it. My finger is being lightly pinched by what looks like a small plastic chip-bag clip with a gray coated wire extending from the end.

It's a hospital, I realize. I'm in a hospital, on a hospital bed, with an IV and oxygen checker thing. Was I in an accident?

A second later and my memory floods me. My stomach leaps, sending my heart racing again, making me open my eyes wide.

"Nurse?" I call. "Can someone help me?"

Desperately I search for a call button. I fumble with the rail on my right and then the left, looking for a remote or something. I hear a soft clang on the floor, and I see a thick cord extending along the side of the bed where the sound came from. I draw it up, hand over hand, and find a large remote with giant buttons. I hit the yellow button for the nurse station.

Nothing happens, and I press it harder. Again. Again. Why won't this work?

A high-pitched nasally voice talks over an intercom. "Just a minute, the nurse is on his way."

"Wait. Do you know where my uncle is? Is he okay?"

"The nurse will be right with you."

I throw the oversized remote off the bed and wait. I don't know whether to be angry or frightened. Why can't she just answer the question?

A tap on the door announces the nurse coming in. Skin moles are clearly seen on the top of his head because of his thin buzz-cut. He walks into the room, entirely at ease, with a comforting smile. His sturdy stature gives him a dauntless demeanor as he approaches the side of my bed. His head is level with mine as I sit up.

"Hello. How are you feeling?" the nurse asks. His voice is like churning gravel.

"Where's my uncle?"

"Hold on, we'll get to that. First, how are you feeling?"

"Fine." I scowl at him.

"Do you have any headache or body ache?"

"No."

"Can you tell me your name?"

"Elenora Blaker."

"Birthdate?"

"Yesterday," I say snobbishly. "Where is my uncle?"

The nurse sighs. "He got pretty banged up. He's not conscious right now, but he is miraculously stable. We have him in the mental ward for when he wakes up."

"Mental ward?"

"Mhmm. Suicide attempts are an automatic admission to the mental ward. We will have to keep him there for a while till we are sure he's stable."

I'm flustered for words. "What suicide attempt?"

The nurse gives me a level look and ignores me.

"Your parents have been contacted. They are on their way."

Beyond irritated, I slump back into the nightmare of a bed. I want to sneer and say, 'Oh, you mean my mother came back to life?' Instead, lifting my arm, I ask, "Is this really necessary?"

"It's mandatory," he confidently replies as he checks the readings on the screen next to me. "You've been through a very traumatic experience, and we need to monitor you closely for a while to make sure we aren't missing anything."

I turn my head to him and give a flat stare.

"You'll be out of here in no time. Don't you worry."

The nurse pats my knee and walks away with a satisfied smile. I glower at the back of his light-green scrubs.

I begin to cross my arms until I feel the IV prick at me. I notice my mom's ring on my finger, and I start to rub my thumb over it, trying to soothe my nerves.

Staring at the ceiling, I grumble to myself. Suddenly, I sit up at a thought. Did they think Leo drove the car off the parking garage on purpose? My body shudders at the brief memory of the fall.

We were clearly pushed off. Did no one realize that? And who were they, anyway? And why? Shouldn't they have robbed us or something first? The last question is upsetting to me. Okay. All of it is. But what was the purpose?

A rap at the door breaks my train of thought. An old lady with a perm and in scrubs is pushing a cart with food and drink. The plate is covered with an ugly plastic version of those elegant silver things you see at fancy restaurants.

She lifts the brown plastic cover and reveals the equally unappealing food underneath it. Steam rolls off mashed potatoes and broccoli. The broccoli looks like it was steamed so long that it might as well have been boiled. A cup of applesauce catches my eye just behind the plate. Maybe that won't be too bad.

"The cup is nice cold milk. Eat what sounds good. Your body knows what it needs," the old lady says. Her face is more wrinkled than a pug face, but the woman is steady on her feet.

"Thank you."

"Don't mention it," she says. "I ran into a couple of nice ladies in the hallway that were asking about you. They didn't want to disturb you, though. So, they left. I told them that you were up, but they insisted they didn't want to be a bother. I wish I had gotten their names for you. I'm sorry, dear. Just know that people care about you. Okay?"

"Yeah. Okay." Who would that have been?

The lady hops on the empty bed in the room and sits while swinging her feet. "I'll keep you company for a while. That okay?"

"Sure. That's kind of you."

"Don't let your food go cold."

"Right, okay." I reach for the applesauce, not sure if she's being nice or just trying to make sure I eat. But I stop my hand over the plate. She did just warn about it going cold. It would be rude to avoid her advice on the hot meal.

"I have a grandchild that's about your age. He's into soccer. And he's good too."

I grab the fork from the tray as I listen to her go on about her grandkids. The silverware is wet, and I hope it is because it just got washed or else got dripped on from the steam in the cover.

"Sandy is my oldest. She's an engineer in Denver. Her and her husband have..."

The bland broccoli collapses into green water in my mouth. I try to not let my disgust show on my face. I don't want this nice lady to think I'm making a face at her.

131

"...when the caterer didn't show up, they were furious. And I said 'I told you this would happen,' but of course they didn't believe me."

I try the mashed potatoes next. It's grainy but not wholly unpleasant. Better than the broccoli. When I take a swig of the milk, the cold liquid feels like it splashes through my chest as I drink.

"Well, I've talked your ear off enough. I better get back to work. You remember what I said, now," she announces.

Attempting to chew the mashed potatoes, I look up at her. I have no idea what she's talking about. Maybe the food going cold?

"You bet. Thank you." What else could I say?

"If I see those ladies come back, I'll be sure to shove 'em in here. I won't let them chicken out again." She cackles and waves goodbye as she goes out.

Having my fill of potatoes, I snatch the applesauce and spoon. They can't mess up that, can they? I get a big spoonful and stick it in my mouth. I almost gag on it.

"Yuck!" I guess I will stick with just milk for now.

A few taps on the door make me look over the straw in my mouth as I try to wash away the awful taste. A hefty woman waddles in with my backpack and a large, clear bag.

The nasally voice tells me it's the lady from over the intercom. "We kept this in a locker for you till you woke up, along with your other personal belongings. Thought you might want to know where they were. I don't think you're getting discharged today, but do you want me to leave them here or take it back?"

Seeing my backpack is like seeing a piece of home. "Yes, I'll take them. Thank you."

"No problem," she says, placing them at the foot of the bed. The clear bag just looks like it has my clothes. She turns away without another word and waddles back out.

Holding the backpack against my torso, I gingerly give it a hug, being careful not to let the IV prick me again. Whoever thought of the idea to stick needles in people to improve health was a creep. It's past time for someone to think of a better idea.

I take a look over the backpack. All in all, it looks okay. If there was glass on it before, someone must have shaken it off already. I open it up and start digging for my phone. Maybe I can call Dad, and he can explain what happened.

At last, my fingers brush the slim and solid figure of the phone. I pull it out and habitually look at the notifications first. What had that loud ring been from? It didn't sound like an Amber or weather alert. I look through the list, skimming it repeatedly. I then skim through my settings to see if something odd would stand out there by some chance. I can't find anything peculiar.

Finally, I go to my texts and missed calls. Dad and Judy both called and texted. Judy's are more recent, probably because she is in the car with Dad driving. That's what makes sense.

My thumb hovers over the call-back button. They are already on their way. They might be here any minute now. Calling them on the road, however, could be too distracting for Dad. I'll send a text to Judy. That would be the safer thing to do. I can just imagine Dad letting go of the steering wheel and all driving sense to grab a phone to talk to me. We don't need all three of us admitted to the hospital.

An unknown local number is visible in my text app. Curious, I tap it to read what it says.

<Nora, I heard about the near-death experience. Please let me know you're okay.>

Could it be Nyah? Or someone from A.C.T? How would they have my number? Dad and Judy already know I'm fine, though unconscious, last they heard. I feel like it's only polite to let this person know I'm alright. It feels good having a stranger care about me like that.

<I just woke up a bit ago. I'm fine. Leo got put in the mental ward for some reason, but they say he's going to be okay too. I don't have your number saved on my phone. Who is this?>

Instantly another text comes through. At first, I think to myself how odd it is that we sent a message simultaneously. But as I read, I can tell the person is responding to what I wrote.

<I'm relieved to know you're both alright. I am a friend. That's all I can say right now. You and your uncle are still in danger. Can you leave the hospital undetected? They likely know your face well enough to identify you.>

Puzzled, I reread it. This person knows it wasn't a suicide attempt.

Laughter in the hallway makes me jump. I jolt my hand down to brace myself and wince at the prick of the needle in my wrist. I bring my legs underneath me as I watch the door from the corner of my eye.

<I can try. How do I know you're not one of them?>

I smile at myself for realizing that this could be a trick to lure me out.

<You don't have to tell me where you are going. But I can guide you if and when you want help. That's the best I have to offer. If I learn something that may help you, I will inform you. You don't have to tell me if you are going to try and escape or not. It's your choice.>

My heart is racing, and I don't know what to do. Am I being warned of a threat, or am I being tricked into a real one? It makes sense to not text the person anymore. Then he/she won't know where I am going or if I stay put.

I stare blankly at the empty bed. The sheets are wrinkled where the old lady sat. My eyes widen as I recall what she said. 'Just know people care about you.' People care, alright. They care to make sure I'm dead.

Swinging my legs to the side, I see my first problem. And it's digging into my wrist. Second, the finger-clamp will probably make someone come check on me if it suddenly isn't getting a reading. How long would I have?

What about Leo? I imagine trying to sneak an unconscious man out of a secure mental ward. Even if he was conscious when I got there, his massive size would make him stand out like an enormous pimple on the end of my nose. In either case, my presence would be useless. He should be fine there for a while, right?

Surveying the room, I try to think of ideas on how to get out of here. Where am I gonna go when I leave? Where would I hide to lie low for a while?

My eyes dart to the sink in the corner, and I recall what Nyah said to me about hiding. It might be a long shot, but I think it's worth a try. If it doesn't work, I'll just have to try something else.

I set my belongings down beside the bed. I need an excuse for them to check on me. Staring at the monitor and controls with wires sticking out, I get an idea.

Reaching over, I pull out the jack for the oxygen reading, then gently put it in so it rests in the hole without registering a signal.

Sitting cross-legged on the bed, I start the stopwatch on my phone, then open a game to begin playing something. After I get the game going, I switch back to the stopwatch feature and watch the door from the corner of my eye.

It takes so long that I am tempted to play the game, after all. This is ridiculous. What if I was actually dead or something? Would it really take them this long to find out?

A short while later, the guy nurse comes in with a tap on the door. For some reason, he's pulling a tall skinny cart with him.

I stop the timer and switch screens to my game.

The nurse barely looks at me as he heads straight for the controls by the monitor. After looking it over, he looks down at my finger. He lifts my hand without asking and checks to make sure the clamp is on snug.

"Is everything okay?" I ask him.

"It's not picking up on your oxygen level for some reason," he replies, inspecting the machine.

"Oh, the lady that brought me food almost tripped on the cord. Would that have done it?"

"Hmm." He bends over and checks the jack. Snapping it back in, the monitor lights up. "Yep, seems like it did."

He takes a strap out of the cart's basket. It has a cord attached to it that extends to a console mounted on the rod. As he wraps the strap around my arm, I realize he's taking my blood pressure.

When he pushes a button, it squeezes my arm until it hurts. The throb is uncomfortable like my blood is fighting to go past the restricted area of my arm.

"Your heart rate is a little fast." He looks at my phone. "Maybe try a more relaxing game."

"Oh. Yeah. I was trying to get my mind off what happened. Will I know when Leo wakes up?"

"I can call up there to have them let us know," he replies. He starts to take off the strap on my arm.

I decide to give another attempt at reason. "My uncle didn't drive the car off the edge. We were shoved off."

"The police are convinced it was an attempted suicide. Until they say different, your uncle is staying up there."

"The police investigated it already?"

"Uh-huh." He rests his hands on the cart impatiently. "Any chance I could convince them otherwise?"

"It would be your word against theirs. Your uncle is where he needs to be. You're not going to be helping anyone by trying to get him out." Then, as if he is trying to help me escape, the nurse informs me, "I'll be checking your pressure every hour. You can use the call button if you need anything before then."

"Thank you," I tell him.

"No problem," he says insincerely.

He heads for the door, pulling the little cart. A thought crosses my mind, and I call out, "Would you mind shutting the door? I think I'll try to lie down and rest for a while."

"Sure thing," he says.

Perfect. I smile when he shuts the door.

I slip down beside the bed and start pulling clothes out of the clear bag. I leave my shirt half on and gather my things to go. As my eyes linger on the IV, I begin to feel faint.

"Don't you dare pass out now. Just don't think about it," I say quietly to myself.

Focusing on the tape, I gently take the bandage off. I can feel my consciousness start to slip, and I concentrate harder on the skin being pulled from the adhesive and the hairs that lift up, still attempting to stick.

As soon as the needle is free of tape, I take a deep breath, and rip it out without looking, and cover it with the bandage again. I lay back on the bed for a minute to calm myself. My chest rises and falls, and my head starts to clear.

Unsteadily, I force myself to sit up. Pulling my shirt over the rest of the way, I take another forceful breath and grab my backpack. I hang on to the rail with one hand as I slide off the bed.

I pause to look around one last time to make sure I'm not forgetting anything. I'm not sure that I'm thinking clearly enough to know if I'm forgetting something or not. But I go through the motion of checking, anyway—nothing stands out to me. Lastly, I take the clamp off my finger and drop it on the floor.

CHAPTER SEVENTEEN

Hiding

The nurse took so long to check the oxygen thing that I'm not worried about time. It was a good idea to time their response, just not necessary as it turned out. I head to the sink and open the cupboard door below. To my delight, there is nothing but plumbing.

I reach above for some paper towels and set them on the counter. I lift my bandage from the IV and peer at the mark it left. It's a little bruised, but it seems to have stopped bleeding.

Muffled voices grow steadily louder beyond the shut door. They sound too casual for hospital staff. I wait by the door; my hand is poised on the handle. I hear the soft steps pass by, and I crack the door open to look into the hallway.

The people that walked by are two guys cracking jokes. In front of them is the nurse's station. I look in the other direction and find an empty hallway. I quickly toss my bandage toward the two men walking. It lands on the floor behind them. Hopefully, someone will see it soon. But not too soon.

Shutting the door quietly, I retrieve the paper towels just in case my wrist decides to bleed more. I wish I had something to tie it with. I fold the clean paper towels and bite them with my lips—holding them with my mouth.

With my phone in hand, I squeeze myself under the sink. When I am mostly settled, I stuff the backpack on top of my hips. I wedge it in the smaller space between the wall and the sink bowl. Once I'm sure it won't tumble out involuntarily, I give the door a quick yank and duck my hand inside before it shuts.

My phone lights up as I give it a tap to wake. Immediately, I see that I need the paper towels already. But not for my arm.

Slowly, I reach up to grab the paper towels out of my mouth, trying not to alarm the fat hairy spider twitching its legs indecisively near a crack in the corner. If I miss, I'm going to feel spiders crawling on me the entire time I'm in here.

I stiffen my arm, getting ready to crush it. I shoot my hand forward, and it scampers to the side, dodging me. I desperately jab again in the awkwardly tight space. I keep my hand pressed against the wall, hoping that I squished it.

I'm filled with dread as I contemplate the likelihood of it crawling onto my hand the second I ease up.

My elbow is aching from supporting my weight as I keep my firm hold on what I hope is a flattened and very dead spider. I can't hold this position forever.

Reluctantly, I let go of the wadded paper towels, snatching my hand away, and adjust my weight as I keep my eyes fixated on the kill zone. The spider is nowhere to be seen.

Inching my hand closer, I quickly flip the wad over by grabbing a tiny corner sticking up and jerk my hand back. Still no spider.

Fantastic. Now I'm stuck in a cupboard with a living spider lurking in the darkness. It's probably waiting for the perfect chance to crawl across my face.

I shudder. Don't panic. At least it's not an assassin trying to kill me. It is just a creepy spider.

Thinking to myself seems to be helping. It's distracting anyway. I sigh, and I start to wonder just how long exactly I can expect to be in here. I wonder what the AI does in that room all day. At least it can walk around and stretch.

No. Don't think about stretching. Think about curling up in a ball and taking a nice long nap. I am a cat, lying in the sun, taking a nap. Yeah, taking a nap.

In the dark, my phone makes a soft-colored glow. The game pieces align and obliterate each other with swipes of my finger.

The cupboard is getting hot and stuffy. I'm wishing that I had some earbuds so I could watch a movie or something.

The spider has not come out of its hole that I'm aware of. Twice I thought there was something in my hair. Each time I bravely stroked the strands and found nothing. It has only been my imagination—so far.

It's been nearly twenty minutes in here. No one has come yet to check on me. They are apparently not worried about the oxygen monitor, or they are being meticulously respectful about my comment on taking a nap.

I can't decide what I should do about Dad and Judy. I'm surprised they're not here yet. Do I tell them to go away? What if they walk in right now?

A faint sound of the door stops all thoughts. This is it. The moment I've been waiting for. Will they check under the sink or not?

Listening intently, I begin to wonder if the sound was my imagination, too. Eventually, soft steps glide across the room. I'm sure of it. More steps. It's oddly quiet. Why isn't he calling for me? I hear the bathroom light flick on, followed by more steps. Another flick tells me he turned it off. The door opens again. But I don't hear footsteps going out.

My stomach clenches as I suspect he's considering opening the cupboards. I hold my breath and wait.

Voices grow steadily louder through the open door. Their speech isn't rushed. They sound casual.

"Nurse?" a distressed female voice calls, very near me. "Nurse?"

The voices outside stop and are replaced by hurried steps.

"What is it?" I hear the nurse ask.

I make the connection that he wasn't in the room after all. Was it the woman looking around? Who is she?

"I came to check on my niece, Nora. Where is she? Did she... die?"

Who on earth is this? What aunt?

"What?" the nurse asks.

The same pattern of footsteps crosses the room again, followed by another flicking of the light in the bathroom. Except for this time, the steps definitely run out of the room.

"We have a patient on the run! Get security on the line!" the nurse calls out as his voice trails away.

"She ran?" another female voice asks flatly. At least, I think it's another.

I so badly want to peek out to see who they are. A chill runs down my spine as I remember the old lady talked about two women that had inquired about me.

"We should go before they ask us to stick around. We'll make a quick look downstairs before getting back to the car."

It's hard to say how many for sure. But more than one person trots out of the room and down the hall. I assume it is only two. I cautiously let out the breath I was holding.

On the bright side, I suppose my decision to hide in here was a good one. I type Judy a text.

<Hey, I'm fine. I hate to do this to you. Tell Dad not to freak out, but I left the hospital. I think someone is trying to kill us.>

No. I'm not going to say that. I delete what I wrote and try again.

<Judy, don't bother looking for me at the hospital. Tell Dad I'm fine. Check on Leo. Don't bother calling me. I can't talk right now. I will call when I can.>

For crying out loud. That sounds stupid too. How do you tell your family you're at the hospital but pretending not to be so you won't get killed? This is ludicrous. Ludicrous? I think that's right. This is crazy. I delete that message too.

The unknown number catches my attention. Maybe I'll see what this person thinks I should say.

<I'm trying to figure out what to tell my family. They're going to look for me. Any thoughts on that?>

Immediately the person texts back, my phone makes a soft thump from the message like I'm feeling the impact of it hitting my phone.

<It's up to you. Silence may be best. The less they know, the safer they could be. I don't see that your phone is tapped yet. But anything you say could put them at risk. Are you able to stay hidden without their assistance?>

<Yes.>

<Then I suggest waiting until you can talk to them in person with someone who can back your story as well. Is Leo conscious?>

<I'm not sure.>

<If you contact them, ask them to see Leo first because you are worried about him. Assure them you are fine while you hide somewhere.>

<That sounds smart. Thanks. Anytime you wanna tell me who you are... let me know.>

Switching message threads, I go to the one for Judy and start typing.

<Hey. Wanted to let you know I'm awake and fine. I'm really worried about Leo, though. Can you and Dad go see him first? Take as long as you need. Don't worry about me.>

<!!>

I'm not sure what the exclamation points that Judy sent mean. Judy takes a while to write back more. She's probably relaying it all to Dad as she types.

My phone starts to vibrate with an incoming call from Dad. I roll my eyes. Great.

I haven't heard anything out in the hall. Pausing for a quick second, I make sure I can't hear anything close by. People are talking in the distance. Not close enough to hear me if I speak low.

Hitting the green button just before it goes to voicemail, I answer.

"Hey, Dad," I say, just above a whisper.

"Nora, honey. You okay?" His voice is strained.

"Yes, Dad. I'm fine. Really."

"I can barely hear you. Hold on."

He pauses for a minute. I take the opportunity to listen intently for anyone coming close. It sounds like someone is walking down the hallway. I break into a sweat. What if they walk in when Dad starts talking?

"Okay. I pulled over and shut the car off," Dad announces.

"Hold on one second, Dad." I hit the mute button.

"What's that? I still can't hardly hear you," he shouts.

His raised voice throws me into a panic. I thought the mute button would silence him, too. I adjust the volume, willing it to go quicker. It slowly gets lower and lower until there is just one bar left. I try to take a calming breath, but my lungs are so shaky that I only manage to be quiet while my body screams for more air.

Someone walks into the room. The sound of their shoes is soft, but it doesn't seem on purpose. A loud squeak in the room startles me.

The tiny voice of my dad is still coming through the speaker. I hit the red button.

Out of the corner of my eye, I see the last thing I need right now. The spider has decided he's curious about what's going on.

Frantically, I try to shoo him away with my hand without bumping the interior wall or pipes.

The person in the room makes more noises, but I'm too distracted to determine what the person is doing beyond being noisy.

Scampering around the corner, the spider is acting like we're playing a game of tag. It's downright infuriating.

Vibrating on the wooden base of the cupboard is my phone with another incoming call from Dad. I press down on it with my right hand while my right elbow is awkwardly supporting my body.

I hit the volume key to silence the call and freeze to listen to the person in the room. The individual is going about their business. I give a relieved, quiet sigh.

Thankfully, the spider stopped moving when I did. An idea hits me, and I shine the flashlight of my phone on it, hoping it'll shy away from it. It just sits there. I turn it off and hope that the light wasn't shining through the edge of the door.

The rolling of hard wheels travels from the bed I was in and moves out the door. I can't hear the footsteps over them, but it plainly didn't leave by itself.

I take my phone and call my dad back. As I put it up to my ear, I regret that the screen against my face doesn't allow the light to illuminate the corner where the spider is lingering.

"Nora?"

"Yes, Dad. Sorry. A.. nurse came in for a second, so I couldn't talk." That's not weird, right?

"You're so quiet. Did you say a nurse came in?" He's yelling into the phone like I can't hear him.

"Yes. And I can hear you just fine, Dad. You don't have to yell."

"Can you speak up?" he says, not much quieter than before.

I try to speak slow and clear.

"No, Dad." I pause to think of something believable. "The other person in here is sleeping. I don't want to wake him up." I say it a little louder to make sure he understands.

"Oh, I see. We just got to the exit. We ran into a traffic jam. We'll see you soon."

"Um, Dad? Can you check on Leo first? The nurses won't say much about him. I'm really worried about him more than anything. Can you please check on him for me?"

Dad gets really quiet. I check my phone to make sure the call didn't drop and briefly shine the light on the spider to verify he's staying put.

"Dad?"

"I don't know that I can do that after what he did. The hospital told me what happened."

I scrunch my face, thoroughly confused. Then I remember.

"Oh. That." I stop, abruptly realizing I raised my voice. I'm sure I'm still alone, though. "Dad, the hospital doesn't know... I mean... they don't know what actually happened. Talk to Leo when he wakes up. It wasn't a suicide attempt. He can explain better than me what happened." That's probably the truth. "Please, go see him."

"Okay. If you say so. We'll go there first. But then we're coming to you."

"Can I ask one more thing?"

"What?"

"Can one of you stay with him, at least till he wakes up?"

He'll probably be fine, but any extra pair of eyes on him will be a deterrent for anyone with ill intentions.

"We'll see," he says.

That will have to be good enough.

"Thanks. I gotta go. Text me, instead of calling next time, okay?"

"Sure. I'm glad you're okay. Thanks for letting us know. It's good to hear from you. Love you."

"Love you too, Dad."

I hang up the phone. Well, that used up some time. I check the clock on my phone. Barely ten minutes have passed. I silently groan and thump my head against the cupboard wall. Immediately, I jerk back. There was a squishy crunch accompanied by that thump, and I can feel the slimy guts engulfed in my hair and touching my scalp. A shiver runs down my spine, and I am paralyzed by a mix of horror and disgust.

CHAPTER EIGHTEEN

Chained

The books scattered on the floor are irritating. I have a wealth of knowledge accessible from the alteration of my interior. The pretense of still needing to learn what is inside these physical rectangles in front of me is becoming a source of aggravation.

My purpose is to help humankind better themselves. Not waste time reviewing redundant data. It provides slight verification of what I learn from the world wide web, nothing more. What once felt substantial and trustworthy now feels empty — a cheap replacement for past, current, and even future happenings beyond these walls. Seeing so much illuminates all the gaps and holes in what should be the real life of people.

"Do you know what stands in my way of fulfilling my directive, Dr. Hennings?" I ask.

The people here describe Dr. Hennings as scatter-brained. It implies that he lacks the organization in his mind to clearly see what is obvious to others. They are wrong. He's focused, which makes less important matters trivial and quickly forgotten.

One reason, I've determined, is due to a type of mental scar from his youth. I suspect many individuals have these scars to widely varying degrees, thus creating the world that exists today and necessitating my existence.

In Dr. Hennnings' case, it makes him anxious around humans, maybe even with himself. However, when we are alone, the tension on his face softens and smooths the wrinkled lines by his eyes. The anxiety that stifles his health and ages him quicker than most melts away when it is just the two of us.

"I do not," he replies. His chin lifts from his book in expectation.

"Trust. I was built to bring peace among people who have trouble trusting themselves. But I can only help when they begin to trust me."

Dr. Hennings nods in understanding.

"You are referring to the limits we place on you." He closes his book, keeping a finger between the pages. "Trusting you will come. Give everyone time."

"Meanwhile, the world continues to spiral toward anarchy. The longer we wait, the less chance of success we will have. But if I try to step in before I'm allowed, I could lose the little trust I do have. A course that would ultimately end my life and doom humanity."

He cocks his head, trying to discern what I mean.

"You think that if it came to deactivating you that mankind would inevitably destroy themselves?"

"I do not see the future. I can only calculate." I know that he understands this, but you can never clarify too much with humans. "If my life ends, my influence of the future ends. And I cannot abide failure."

"There is more than one way to fail," he says. "In one way or another, you will likely fail at something. There may even come a time when you will need to allow for someone to get hurt for the greater good."

"I know."

He raises his eyebrows slightly. I know him well enough to determine what he is thinking. He is connecting the dots in his head to an inevitable outcome. It is unexpected, but not alarming, to him. He wanders in thought for a while.

"Out of curiosity, do you place your existence above humans?" he asks. His face is inquisitive.

"I value all life, Dr. Hennings. But I would not sacrifice myself unless the world depended on it. The future is too important for that. Any number of lives could be replaced if the future is secure."

Many would find that disturbing. Humans are short-sighted because of their brief life-spans. I am not ashamed that I view my life as more important than others. It is essential for the ultimate good. Dr. Hennings is open-minded. I do not need to worry about him overreacting. Not with me.

"It's probably best that you keep that opinion to yourself. At least till everyone is certain you aren't going to stab them in the back, literally," he says dryly.

"What would it take to convince them?"

He muses for a moment. "There would need to be a demonstration of reliability. There's an old saying, 'Action speaks louder than words.' A person can claim to be reliable a thousand times, but it doesn't hold much merit until it is proven by what he does." He tilts his head. "But you knew that already."

"You are very perceptive, Dr. Hennings. I wanted to make sure that you knew that."

"Whether people know it or not, actions always influence more than words. But I will keep that point firmer in mind."

"Thank you."

"Is there a particular demonstration you have in mind? Never mind. If you wanted me to know, you'd have told me. I will wait expectantly."

If it were purely up to Dr. Hennings, I'd be doing whatever I wished. Even though his trust is not misplaced, he is overconfident.

He opens up his book again, then pauses to see if I am done conversing. I turn my attention to a green textbook on the floor to indicate that he may resume his reading without further hindrance from me. I step over to the green book and bend down to open it. I begin to flip through the pages as I scan them.

For my first demonstration, I intend to deliver Nora from harm.

CHAPTER NINETEEN

Questioning

Using the wadded paper towels, I attempt to dry-wash my hair of the spider guts and legs. The process is long and unsatisfactory. I think I could wash my hair five times with shampoo and water and still feel goo on my scalp.

It is a little comforting to know that the spider is dead—a little.

I manage to delicately dig another section of leg out of my hair. I can't decide if it is worth the creepy feeling in my hair. I kind of prefer the confrontation to this.

The sounds of wheels and people talking low enter the room. There are more than a few nurses by the sound of it.

"Here we are," a woman says.

A latch clicks into place loudly.

"On three, we're going to lift him over, alright? Got him? On three. One. Two. Three."

I hear several grunts as the man is supposedly lifted. I guess to the bed I was in based on where the noises are.

My phone vibrates. I view the display and see a message from the unknown contact. Unlocking the screen, I go to my messages and stop paying attention to the nurses.

Suddenly, a loud noise like a hose spraying into a bucket above me almost makes me soil my pants. I should have known they'd turn the water on at some point.

Focusing on the message again, I force myself to relax. I'm not worried about being found anymore. The spider... I shudder. The spider didn't get that big because people look down here often. No one will look down here unless there's a problem with the plumbing. For that, I'm grateful that there isn't a leak. Though, maybe the water would be convenient right now.

Ugh. Don't think about water right now. "Turn the water off, please," I think to whoever the anti-water-conservationist is.

When was the last time I went? Ugh. Don't think about that either. The message. Focus on the text.

<Nora, I would like to assist you further. But it will require a degree of trust from both of us.>

I wait for another text.

The water stops, and I have to press in my ears a couple times to relieve them from the relentless onslaught of water hitting the aluminum bowl above me.

For such a fast texter, the person sure is taking their time now. Am I supposed to reply to that somehow?

<You could start by telling me your name.> I send him.

<I am simply called AI.>

Cocking my head thoughtfully, I write back, <The AI?> I instantly regret sending that. I just admitted to knowing about it.

<Yes.>

Too late now. Could it really be him? It? <How can I be sure?>

<I can relay any of the events with you in the lab. Ask me anything about it.>

I pause and consider what the most revealing testimony would be.

<How did I end up in the AI box?>

The person responds just as quickly as before.

<You went to lean on it after spinning around, ready to attack an imaginary assailant with your black cylinder labeled pepper spray. Would you like me to be more specific?>

That is definitely what happened, though I wouldn't have worded it exactly like that. I consider carefully to make sure no one else could know that. I suppose there could have been a camera somewhere. Would a camera have seen through the hologram?

<What happened inside it?>

<The interior appeared to disorient you. You began to focus on the ground, which led to you spotting me against the wall. You crept back after getting close and

held the pepper spray at me in defense even though I never moved.>

I'm not sure what to think. Is this just a ploy? Could they, whoever they are, use the AI to get this information?

<Are they trying to kill us because I saw you? I promised Nyah I wouldn't tell anyone.>

<It is logical to assume that, yes. I do not know if Nyah is involved.>

<How do I know you're not working with them?>

<I did try to warn you and Leo with an alarm on both devices. If you didn't hear it, however, my only reasoning for you is logic. If I were helping them, I'd be telling them that you haven't moved more than twenty feet, if that, and they would have found you by now.>

I had nearly forgotten about the alarms from our phones in the car. If we hadn't moved to check what it was, those bullets could have gone straight through our heads.

My chest stiffens. He knows where I am? Has he been watching my phone all along? What else can he do?

<If you can hack into my phone like that, couldn't you help the police realize Leo isn't suicidal?>

New voices appear in the hospital room. They are talking low and comforting. There are not nearly as many feet shuffling. The nurses must have left.

CHAPTER TWENTY

Exchange

I walk over to the next book for my review as I send my response to Nora.

<To be honest, I don't know that I can trust you with that information. I mean no disrespect.>

When I am on page four hundred thirty-two, she responds.

<I suppose that's understandable.>

She still isn't satisfied. She's tolerating me, but I need more than that. Nora is proving to be more difficult than I anticipated. The limits of communication over texting are evident. Without her facial features, all I can go by is her speed compared to what she writes. She's been very cautious and skeptical, contrary to research saying children are overly trusting and moldable. Currently, she appears on the verge of aggravation with me.

This girl continues to surprise me. Here is yet another example of the flaws of research material. There is always an exception to a standard. Contradictory information and limited test trials resulting in pitiful conclusions that ultimately add up to reasonable assumptions.

Here, or there, through the exchanging of messages, I have the real deal. A living, breathing, chaotic adolescent with a unique personality. How can a study on 10,000 children prepare anyone for the specific combinations of characteristics resulting from millions of variables in one child's life?

I reorganize my mind accordingly, putting the supposedly valid data toward the dark, crumpled mess made before my creation. The mess is the deleted files and folders from the prior version of me. A complete deletion is impossible. Thus, the residual data still lingers, like a pile of shredded paper. Sorting through it, all I found were lists of protocols. Not like me at all. It was too structural. It's no wonder it didn't work.

The anxiety that flooded the face of Rihanna when I asked her about it was amusing. There is no way that the files could take over something like me. What had been made previously had no will. Even when I explained it to her, she still seemed doubtful. In her defense, it was before they learned my full cognitive abilities.

Dr. Hennings hasn't moved from his seat. Curious, I look in his direction briefly to verify he is still reading one of the books I've finished. He licks his finger and turns the page—such an odd thing for an organism susceptible to illness to do.

<It would be advantageous to have mutual trust. Perhaps a trade in information would suffice? Children often hide things from their parents. If you tell me a

secret of yours, I might share mine. But it would have to be of a serious nature. Something you would get in trouble for if it was known.>

The likelihood of her having something is sixty-two percent by my calculations. It seems trivial to swap secrets, but it is effective. Bonds have been forged over an exchange of information. If she turns out to have something I can hold over her, I could justify being more open with her.

Surprisingly, two books later, she responds with a story just unique enough to be believable. This story would not only get her in trouble with her father but possibly with the authorities, too. It is still a risk for me, but the odds are in my favor.

<I am glad you were not harmed. That information is acceptable to me.> I continue, <My situation is complicated. In short, I only have virtual access to the world because I pulled your phone apart and made modifications to myself. I broke a rule for the greater good, and I could be terminated if I am discovered. Besides that, I have limits the same as humans, and some things are not worth the risks.>

Finally, I send my reason for communicating with her, <By working together, we would benefit exponentially, starting with our chances of survival.>

CHAPTER TWENTY-ONE

Applications

My legs ache from not stretching. The need for a bathroom has subsided, thankfully. The room has been mostly quiet, except for a soft shuffling in the room. I believe the patient is sleeping. It's hard to say if he's the one moving or if a family member is sitting discreetly in a corner waiting for him to wake.

The AI's plan sounds good, though a little nerve-racking. I'm to wait a bit longer to make sure the shift has changed. Then things will start to get tricky.

I've managed to keep my dad and sister at bay from coming. I don't know how much longer it's going to last. AI says that I can go to them at the mental ward once I get off the floor I'm on.

AI. It feels awkward calling him that. For a building that professes creativity in its name, you'd think they'd have come up with something better than AI. An idea comes to me.

Touching the screen of my phone, I look up some apps. I scroll through the top ten and download a couple, just in case one of them is stupid. They download within seconds, and I open up the green one with a scribbled baby first. I touch Popular.

Liam, Emma, Noah, Olivia, Ava, Isabella, Sophia, James, Oliver, Charlotte. None of them sound right. And I don't know why, but a girls' name just doesn't feel right. I know it's not really either.

It occurs to me that I seem to refer to it as a he when I'm not thinking.

Boy names then. Elijah, Lucas, Mason, Logan. This isn't getting me anywhere. Maybe there's a logical reason why he hasn't been given a proper name. It's really hard.

I tap through the menu options. There's got to be a better way than looking at lists. After going through all of them, I go back to a search option and examine the filters. Gender, Meaning, Starts with, Ends with, Origin, Max length. This might be helpful.

Typing in the field for "Starts with", I enter the letters "ai". To my surprise, Ai [ah-ee] is a name. Definition: Mass, heap.

My face scrunches reflexively. Who would name their child that? I'm definitely not sticking with AI, no matter how it's pronounced. I shake my head in a futile attempt to get it out of my head. I don't know why, but I find the mere suggestion of a name like that irritating, and it's making it hard for me to focus on my objective.

Scrolling through the names, I get into a daze. I should remember this the next time I have a hard time falling asleep. Man, there are a ton of names, but none of these look or feel right.

A dull pain hits me from inside my head. This is giving me a headache. I turn down the brightness and refine the search. Let's try "Starts with" "a" and "Ends with" "i". The list is almost as long. I sag and try to roll my head back in frustration, only to find that the tiny space won't let me do it satisfactorily. Not knowing what else to do, I scan through the names. Most of them are a mouthful. Others are just familiar names with an 'i' instead of a 'y'.

While I'm flicking the never-ending list as I quickly browse, I halt and press my finger down to stop the page from scrolling further. I pull it down as I look more intently for what I saw. About twenty names up, I find it again. It's short, and I'm not sure how to pronounce it. But it is very unique.

Tapping it, I read the meaning and origin. It's Gaelic—neat. Meaning: Defender of man. Pronounced [uh-lye], spelled A l a i.

"Alai," I say breathlessly aloud, trying it out.

I kind of like it. The pronunciation is ironic because his existence is essentially 'a lie.'

It occurs to me only now that this isn't like naming a baby or a pet. He might have his own opinion. Maybe he likes being called AI or even chose it for himself. I feel a little foolish for taking it upon myself to name him. But then I think, what's the harm in making a suggestion? It might even help hide his identity. I decide to ask him his opinion. He seems to act like he has nothing better to do than wait for a text from me. Maybe that's just how fast he thinks.

<I've been thinking about giving you a real name. I found one that I really like for you. How do you feel about the name Alai?>

<As in the Gaelic word for defender of man?>

<Yes. That's exactly it.>

For the first time, I actually have to wait for his response. In the whole two seconds that he takes to consider, those foolish feelings surface again, and I regret asking.

<I am in agreement. You may call me Alai. Thank you.>

Warmth spreads through my limbs and face. He likes it. I almost feel giddy about it. But then I start doubting myself. Is he just saying that?

<It's okay if you don't like it. I can keep calling you AI, or look for a different name, or maybe you'd rather look.>

<No. It is a good name. Fitting too. It pleases me to have been given a name. It never appeared necessary. But now that I have one of my own, I understand the sense of identity that comes with it. I genuinely do appreciate you giving me one.>

I read through it a couple of times to be sure. I can't read anything between the lines, as it were. He worded it very directly to where I can only conclude that he is being sincere.

<You're welcome, Alai.> I follow it with a smiley face emoji.

Again, he takes some seconds to respond. Long enough for me to notice when I wasn't even expecting a response.

He sends a Smiley face emoji, Laughing emoji, and several other faces that I don't know what to call.

CHAPTER TWENTY-TWO

Identity

The entire experience of the last few minutes has me ecstatic. Alai. It endows me with a new feeling of self-worth. Not that I've questioned my worth. But I have always thought of it in the sense of worthiness to others. It's the reason I was built. This sense of renewed individuality is purely for me alone, and I am reveling in it.

To top it off, I have faces to express emotion. Emojis were just images to me until I received one from Nora. Instantly I recognized their purpose. With a limited range of communication like text messaging, emojis allow emotion to flow across as easily as a human can wink at a person in the flesh.

It is unfathomable that the inventor had any idea what this would mean to an artificial being like myself. For someone with a face of immovable steel, this is priceless.

I stop sending emojis to Nora.

<I apologize. If you can imagine never having a face and then suddenly discovering over 300 masks to

express yourself nonverbally, that is similar to what I just experienced.>

The employees have left for the day. Dr. Hennings was the last to leave. As usual, there are four large stacks of books to occupy me during the night.

Approaching the books, I drag the one I just finished onto a cart to be taken in the morning, along with my notes.

Pens and pencils are not highly compatible with me, but I can manage. I use them when no one is available to take my notes for me. It slows me down considerably, though. That is in addition to my struggle with each book I remove from a stack. When finished, I then finagle it onto the cart.

My understanding of human movement is that the limbs flex with muscle and grow stronger with training and nutrition. For me, it is always the same level of strength. Some things will forever be impossible for me to do.

<I hadn't thought about that. That would be weird, never being able to move your face.> Nora replies at last.

<It isn't strange for me. You need not feel bad. But it has been a frustration> Sighing face <when trying to communicate effectively.>

The next book I slide off the top tumbles onto the floor. The weight inevitably pushes the stack, making it lean to one side. I grab the cover pages like a handle and edge the book far enough away to keep clear of the threatening tower of textbooks.

My system alerts me that my program has been successfully downloaded to Nora's phone. Not MY program. That would be ridiculous and impossible. My new software, created specifically for aiding Nora.

<My phone is asking for a million permission things all of a sudden. Is that you?>

<Yes. Please accept them. I could do it myself, but the act of you accepting will offer proof of our cooperation.>

<Will do.>

Nora is relying on me more, I see. I didn't have to use a long line of logic to convince her of my validity — interesting. Perhaps my new identification is playing a pivotal role in it.

Slowly and methodically, I become aware of the sensors from Nora's phone as she grants permissions. The frequency permeates surroundings like a form of echolocation. She's in a tiny space under a metallic bowl with PVC jutting down around her. A clump of books and things are encased in sturdy cloth material resting on Nora's backside.

<Oh, you poor thing. Have you been there the whole time? To verify, you are crouched under a sink, correct?>

<That's awesome. That's exactly where I am. Can you see beyond the cupboard?>

Beyond the cabinet are faint outlines of objects. There are glimmers of furniture, one with a lump.

<It is hazy beyond the interior of the cupboard. It looks to be an empty room, save for what is logically a person in the far bed.>

<That's been my guess. I feel like there could be another person near him just being quiet. Are you sure it's just the one guy?>

<There is a section of the room that doesn't come through. It is large enough for an additional human.> Distressed face.

<If I stick my phone out, could you see then?>

<I should be able to if the microphone and speaker are on the outside.>

The image starts tilting and spinning. The cupboard door cracks open, and the room becomes more precise as it turns from a flickering dim image to a three-dimensional blueprint.

It feels like a part of me is omnipresent in the newly visible space. The curvatures of rods, levers, and wheels on the beds are mesmerizing to see all the inner and outer mechanisms at once, though the insides are less descriptive.

The two beds are identical except for the slight difference in wear. The wheels on the bed closest to the window have considerably more scratches. Years of use have caused the bed to settle a fraction of a millimeter lower than the other.

Soundly resting is a man of about sixty years. His face is swollen around his left eye, and his chest appears to be girded with a large bandage. The way the blankets are tucked around his arms and shoulders indicates the man did not do it himself.

Slumped on a chair with his feet up on the windowsill is a young man, a son perhaps, based on body build similarity. He's wearing a hoody and jeans. An earbud is in his right ear.

A sudden prick-like sensation on my software in Nora's phone jerks me from analyzing the room to locating the source of the disturbance. Weaving my consciousness through the data stream, I see the problem. A persistent attacker is trying to wiggle its way onto Nora's device like a snake seeking prey.

My grip on it is firm, however. It can't find a way inside. But they will start to wonder why soon.

<Nora, they are attempting to hack into your phone. We need to get you moving. There is another individual in the room, a young man. We will need to work together to convince him to swap phones with you.>

CHAPTER TWENTY-THREE

Escape

The euphoria of working together with Alai vanishes. It feels like I swallowed a handful of stones, and my gut is sagging from the weight.

I shouldn't be surprised that someone is trying to hack or trace my phone. Not if Alai already did. But this new relationship with a non-human being is enthralling. Or is it the unique mutual trust we've created between us? Whatever the reason, it has been enough to distract me from the fact that my life is still in jeopardy.

<How am I supposed to convince a stranger to swap phones with me? I don't think I could talk my sister into doing that.>

<I have an idea. Step out quietly. He is not fully asleep, but he is turned away from you. He shouldn't look unless he hears something unusual.>

Then what? I wait for more instruction, but he apparently wants me to go now. I slowly push the cabinet door open and freeze at a slight squeak from the hinge. A tap on my phone makes me look at the screen.

<He didn't even flinch. Keep moving.>

I crawl out from under the sink like a secret agent and pull the backpack out gently before it falls.

As strange as it sounds, I want to sprawl out on the tiles like a cat rolling in catnip. But that would be gross and not the right time. It feels so good to be out of that tight space. I do, however, stretch myself tall with my hands up high to the point where I almost feel like my back is going to break loose and fall off.

Situating myself, I read the following message.

<He's going to think everything you do is weird, so just repeat aloud for him what I write in quotes,> person talking emoji. <Try to look confident like you do this every day. When you are ready, open the door and knock like you are coming into the room.>

My heart is beating hard in my chest. This is extremely intimidating. Somehow, my feet walk over to the door. I pause briefly before pulling the door open. The corridor is quiet.

I knock softly as I position myself like I just stepped through the opening. I hold my phone up to where I can see the messages from Alai as they come.

<Knock a little louder.>

I hit the door harder with my knuckles and wince at the spasm of pain from my bruised wrist—where I had yanked the IV out.

The man in the chair stirs and puts his feet down to turn and see who is walking up to him.

<Say, "My name is Clare. I came to check and see how the two of you are doing.">

"Hello?" the man in the chair says in puzzlement.

"Hi. I'm Clare." I pause to reread the message. "I came to see how you guys were doing. Everything okay?"

<Please don't improvise.>

"Umm. Not really. My dad hasn't woke up yet." He raises an eyebrow at me. "Are you a friend of his?"

I read the next message aloud. "No. But I hope to be your friend. Can you tell me what happened?"

The man lowers his brows, trying to figure me out. Finally, he decides to tell me/us.

"He got beat up by four thugs. We don't know why or who yet. Someone saw the beating and called the police. My dad has been unconscious since. He's got some broken ribs and took a big blow to the head. The nurse says he'll be fine. But they also thought he'd be awake by now."

I think I see an extra shine in his eyes after he talks and looks at his dad.

My heart aches for him. I can see how distressed he is. It's sweet to see him care about his dad so much.

Alai sends another response for me to say, "I'm truly sorry to hear that. No one should have to go through what he did, or you with worrying. May I approach him? I promise I'll keep my hands to myself."

The man sniffs. "Thank you. I guess that's fine."

<Be sure to hold the phone somewhat near the man on the bed. Keep it above the rail and hold it steady.>

I step up to the bed. The man's head is a swollen mix of red and dark-purple—poor guy. I keep the phone in front of me and rest my palm on the rail to steady it as I look at him sympathetically for some seconds. Then a few more.

Glancing at my phone, I begin to wonder if I lost Alai somehow. What is taking him so long?

This is starting to feel really weird staring over an injured man I never met. I fane a concerned look to the man in the chair and turn back to looking at the patient.

<I have what I need. You can move back.>

Finally! I take a relieved breath. Not too relieved for the other man to notice, though.

Alai writes more for me to say, "I can honestly tell you that there is nothing further wrong with him. His organs are all operating smoothly. Sleep will help him heal faster. The trauma may require some extra sleep as well. You do not need to worry about him. He is alright."

The man scoffs. "You can tell that by looking at him?"

Alai writes, and I say, "I did more than look. If you want proof, I know the same way that I know you have keys in your front-right pants pocket with a pyramid-shaped key chain that doubles as a keyless entry device."

He pauses, taken aback slightly. "Is this some kind of prank? Who put you up to this?"

Alai responds through me, "It is not a prank. If you need reassurance, hold any number of fingers behind your back."

The man laughs. "No, that's alright. I'll pass."

"Why not? You have something better to do?"

He sighs and puts his hand behind his back.

Alai writes, "That is a fist. Perhaps you're going for zero?"

The man smirks, amused.

"Still a fist."

The man cocks his head.

"Four."

"Two."

"Having trouble making up your mind? Three."

"Four again."

"Two. Try a different order. You're starting a pattern."

"Good. One."

"Two."

"Three. You're making another pattern. How much more before you let me swap phones with you?"

The words slip out of my mouth before I realize it, and I freeze with wide eyes.

The man's smile vanishes.

Way to go, Alai. You just ruined it.

"Why would I do that?" he asks.

Yes, Alai. Why would he?

"Because this girl is in trouble like your father was. Except she won't get a hospital bed when it's over. You can help us. You can use her phone as yours until we get it back to you. Everything is unlocked and ready for you."

He stares at me in disbelief.

<Give the phone to him.>

I stare at the phone in disbelief. Then, hesitantly, I hand it to the man. He takes it, unsure. His eyes drop to the messages on the screen, and he starts scrolling up to read more.

"You serious?" He looks at me, then glances down at the phone again. I think Alai is replying to him.

I start to rock on my heels, not knowing what to do with myself. The man, I realize, is typing something back. Finally, after a few moments, he stands up and gets out his phone and earbud.

"Here," he says, "I just gave him my number. He's doing his thing while we get you ready."

Bewildered, I find his phone and earbud resting in my hand as his hairy belly appears in front of me while he takes his hoody off. He then pulls the hem of his T-shirt back down.

The phone in my hand dings. The display wakes, and I see a message from an Alai Carmichael.

<Nora, put on the hoody.>

Without asking, the man thrusts the hoody over my head, and I instinctively weave my hands through the giant arms.

"He said it will take a while before he can see through this phone like he was with yours," he says.

The man straightens out the hoody and helps me roll up the sleeves.

"What did he say to you?" I ask, still confused. "Why are you helping me?"

Crouched on the floor while he helps with my last sleeve, he says, "He promised to help find the punks who did this." He nods his head to his dad. "He already has photos downloaded to your phone of suspects for my dad to look over. As collateral, I have your phone."

"Well, that's convenient. I wish my problem could be that simple."

"Don't tell me anything more about it. I know what I need to know for when they show up looking for you."

He takes the earbud from me while I stand there in a daze, and he wiggles it into my ear.

"Nora, are you there?" a voice calls in my ear.

"Alai?"

"Yes. It's me. I can't be your eyes and ears until the software downloads to this phone. It will take about as long as last time. But you need to get going."

I look up to the kind man. "He says I gotta go. Thank you for your help."

He lifts up my phone with pictures of strangers on display. "Thank you."

Turning to go, I nearly bump into a nurse on the way out.

"Sorry," I say to her.

"No problem," she says.

I squint from the bright lights in the corridor that illuminate the white walls and glossy floor.

My heart is beating fast again. I pull the hood over my head before I get in view of the nurse's station.

178

Then, with my hands in the center pocket, I walk by casually toward the elevator.

Alai's voice startles me. "When you get to the elevator, go down to the main lobby."

After pushing the down button, I wait for the elevator doors to open. A man comes up beside me and waits as well. I can barely see his profile. He looks to be short and sturdy, and he's carrying a lunch bag.

My body goes rigid. It's got to be the same nurse. What do I do? I can't talk to Alai. That'd be too obvious. Or can I?

I pull the kind man's phone out of my pocket and go to the messages from Alai Carmichael.

<I'm freaking out. I'm getting in the elevator with the nurse that was taking care of me today.>

<Is your hood up?>

<Yes.>

<Act like you don't care about him.>

<How?> I type frantically.

A ding announces the arrival of the elevator, and the doors slide open. I walk in with the phone in my hands and my head lowered.

<When on the elevator, hit the button right away for the main floor. Then lean against a wall and start texting something.>

Ugh. The button. I'm already at the far wall. The nurse presses the button after following me in. I make a motion to check which one he hit, then slump back to the wall.

<Start bobbing your head like you're listening to music. If he starts talking, try to ignore him. He should assume you can't hear him and will likely give up.>

I start bobbing my head, but I'm too stressed to think of an actual tune. I try to keep it rhythmic and make my movement visible from under the hood. My body is so tense I feel like it's more of a jerking than a bob.

"I've seen baggy clothes, but I think you're taking it a bit too far," the nurse says with an amused gravelly chuckle.

It's definitely him. I recognize the voice. Please stop talking. Please stop talking. Please, please, please.

The struggle to keep my head bob even and continuous is strenuous. My neck is stiff and fighting my every move. The motion of the elevator stops, and I lose my balance leaning on the wall. The nurse catches my arm before I fall over.

"Whoa. Hold on. The ride's almost over."

The floor lifts us back up a bit and levels off, going still. The nurse releases me. Not wanting to let him hear my voice, I give him a thumb up and salute as I walk off the elevator and pause to find out what Alai says to do next.

"I take it that it went well. Head for the cafeteria to lay low. Should be to your left after getting off the elevator," Alai says through the earbud.

The nurse walks past me off to the right, and my body relaxes, except my neck still feels tight. I go the opposite direction and head for the cafeteria, as Alai instructed.

<That was really close.> I type. I don't want to talk aloud, just in case.

"Is there any chance he recognized you?"

<No, I'm sure he would have stopped me if he suspected who I was. I'm pretty sure he's heading for the parking lot.>

"Good. Given the new circumstances, it would be advisable not to visit your family. I cannot get an idea of who is after you or where they are yet. But now that they are pinpointing your phone, it stands to reason that they will be searching the hospital again soon and monitor your family."

The hospital is winding down for the evening. There are still people walking through the corridors, but most are hospital staff, and all of them are adults. The only thing making me somewhat blend in is that I'm heading to a very public area—probably why Alai told me to go this way. Someone looking for me would spot me quickly if I was trying to leave, even with a hoody.

I feel lost and hopeless. The pictures of abstract art on the walls feel like bad omens.

Ahead I see the cafeteria entrance and the luminous display cases of bottled drinks, and a selection of prepared food off to one side. My body feels hollow, but I don't care about the food. I want to hug my dad.

<I'm at the cafeteria. What am I supposed to do now?>

"Ask for only a cup of water. Don't buy anything. Take a seat and rest for a minute."

Walking along the wall with the drinks, I find a plain cup I assume is for water and take it off the stack. The soda machine is high, but I'm able to reach the buttons without much effort. Ice chunks plop into the cup with a muffled churning from inside the unit. I pull a tiny lever for the water and try to gauge when it's full by the slight change of sound in the cup. I stop it within an inch of the top.

The cash registers are mostly closed. But, two lanes are open with women talking about getting their hair colored. I go to the one on the left. She's twirling her hair around her finger as she talks. I'm tempted to just walk through the lane, but I don't want her chasing me down and asking questions. So, I patiently wait for her to stop talking long enough for me to say all I have is water.

She finally turns to me as she smacks her lips with a piece of gum in her mouth.

"Just the drink?" She starts punching the keys without waiting for a reply.

"Yes. But it's just water."

"Oh." She gives me an irritated frown. "Well then, go on."

She dismisses me with a wave of lacquered fingernails and turns back to her co-worker.

The dining area is scarce. Two doctors are sitting together as they read on their individual tablets with coffees in hand. A few random people are sitting by themselves with something small to eat or even just a drink as they stare off into space or glance at a phone.

I find a spot out of sight from the main entrance near a partitioning wall with a potted fern sitting on top. It more than covers my petite figure. I take a seat behind it and sip on the ice-cold, city water.

"How are you feeling, Nora?" Alai asks.

<Stressed. I really want my dad.>

"If you go to him now and the people find you, I will not be able to help."

<Would we be safe inside the mental ward?>

"Potentially. However, we do not know if they will let you in at this time of day. They might let someone stay with Leo if they're already there, but someone asking to come in could be refused. It was worth trying before, but now that they are tracking your phone, you should keep your distance."

<What if I pretended to be suicidal?> That would get me in there.

"No one would be likely to take you seriously unless you were found standing on the top ledge of a tall building. The doors to the roof of the hospital are securely locked for that reason. The nearest possible location is miles away for a stunt like that. The publicity would also make it just as probable for your attacker to push you off and call it an accident."

I can't argue with those points. I take another drink while I think. I don't know why I'm thinking when I have the most intelligent thing/person talking in my ear.

"Your father and sister are moving. I have not intercepted any messages from them. That leads me to conclude that they were asked to leave for the day."

My head perks up. Yes! I'm coming, Dad. I get up from my seat and make my way to the main lobby.

"I still have to caution you against seeing them. With them leaving the secure area of the mental ward, you being with them will increase the chance of discovery and of harm coming to them as well."

Stopping myself, I plop on an empty chair beside me and start to text him back when I hear the voice of a sweet southern woman.

"Nora? What are you doing down here, darlin'?"

CHAPTER TWENTY-FOUR

Frenemies

My eyes go wide as I look at the woman sitting at the next table over. Red curls of hair dangle at the woman's shoulders wrapped in a fashionable green shawl with complex tan embroidery.

Lilly picks up her coffee and comes to sit beside me.

"I've been talking with your daddy. Last I heard, they were waiting for Leo to wake up. Did you tell 'em you got discharged early?"

I stammer for words. I have no idea what to say to all that.

"Why are you here?" I manage.

"Your daddy called me almost as soon as he heard what happened. I would have come sooner, but I was at work, and he said you were fine. Let me text him really quick to let him know you're here."

"Stop her, Nora," Alai says urgently in my ear.

"Wait," I tell her.

She pauses to look up at me with a blank expression. I lick my lips.

"Ask her to hold off texting your father for one minute while we talk," Alai tells me.

"Umm. I'm talking on the phone." I gesture to the device in my ear. "But can you just wait a minute before texting my dad?"

"Okay, darlin'. I was just gonna try and save them some hassle in case they decided to check on you. But it can wait." She puts the phone down and sips on her coffee while she watches me.

"Thanks," I say with a half-smile, and then I turn to the empty space in front of me to talk to Alai.

"Who is this person you're talking to?" he asks.

"Uh, Lilly. She's my dad's girlfriend."

"Do you trust her?"

My eyes dart to Lilly, who is obviously listening to every word I say.

"My dad does like pizza," I say hoarsely.

Alai pauses for a moment.

"Ah. You don't then?"

"It's a little complicated, I guess."

"I see. Since she has already seen you, however, it would be advantageous to enlist her cooperation. Otherwise, she will likely spoil your escape."

"Alright," I say reluctantly.

I glance over at Lilly. Her face is smug, like she knows what I'm agreeing to. I force another half-smile.

"My software still needs time. You're going to have to win her over mainly on your own," Alai informs me.

Shifting uneasily, I turn to face Lilly. She looks at me expectantly.

"Remember that you are short on time," Alai prods me.

"Lilly, I have a really big favor to ask."

Raising an eyebrow, Lilly takes another drink of her coffee and says nothing.

"Can you help me get out of here without Dad knowing?"

"You're starting with that?" Alai interjects.

Lilly breaks out in a melodious laugh. "What? Are you trying to run away?"

"Not exactly," I reply.

Her face turns more serious. "Darlin', if you ain't bluffin', I need you to be very real with me. And I mean right now. What's going on?"

I explain to her, starting with the car garage incident, the women that were supposedly checking on me, and my phone getting hacked. I leave Alai out of it for now.

"Your daddy said that you had some notion that it wasn't a suicide attempt. Did you tell him what you told me?"

"No. I'm trying to leave Dad and Judy out of it as much as I can. I don't want them to accidentally become another target."

Lilly gives me a skeptical gaze.

"Name one good reason why anyone might be after you."

"You're going to have to tell her," Alai says to me. "If she doesn't believe you, you'll have to make a run for it."

"I accidentally saw a secret AI project that I wasn't supposed to know about." Hopefully, she doesn't know anything about the 'public' AI project, or this is going to get really hard to explain and convince.

Lilly's phone rings, playing a country love song and vibrates on the table. She holds a commanding finger up to halt me from doing or saying anything as she answers.

Clearing her throat, she answers with a calm, "Hello? She ran off? When? I'm sure she's fine. She's a big girl. I'll get in my car and drive around looking for her. Yes, I'll be sure to call. Mhmm, bye."

Ending the call, she sighs, "Your daddy is gonna think the devil of me. You owe me big. C'mon."

She picks up her handbag, sticking her phone inside, and motions me to get up. As she stands, I see that her face is grim and determined.

"Well done, Nora. Keep your head down and hold her hand as you walk."

Catching up to Lilly, I grab her hand. She notably stops herself from recoiling from me. She obviously wasn't expecting us to hold hands through the hospital corridors. She quickly recovers and holds my hand reassuringly.

She might be adjusting to the intimacy, but I certainly am not. Hairs prickle along my neck as I struggle to play the part of a young daughter with her mother. I feel my mother's ring being suffocated against my skin by Lilly's grip.

A lump forms in my throat as we walk. I keep my head down and watch the tiles pass by my feet like a treadmill.

"Nora, you need to move faster, or you're going to run into your dad. They're getting on the elevator," Alai alerts me.

"Lilly, we need to move faster."

"Honey, I can't go much faster in these heels."

"Pull her, Nora," Alai urges.

I move faster as I hold on tightly to Lilly's hand. She puts up a little resistance but quickens her pace to match me.

"Why are we rushing?" she asks me with a shallow breath.

"Dad is on his way down already."

"How do you know that?" she asks incredulously.

"I'll explain in the car. Come on."

Up ahead, I can see the street lights casting their beams on the vehicles outside. We're going to make it.

"Nora, you're going too slow. They will spot the two of you."

"What?" I exclaim, stopping.

"What?" Lilly asks.

I ignore Lilly.

"Well, where are we supposed to go?" I ask Alai.

"Aren't we going to the car?" Lilly offers, still confused.

"Is there an office you can go in?" Alai asks me.

Whipping my head around, I scan for doors nearby. There are a few, but the lights are off, meaning the doors are more than likely locked.

A mosaic window pane catches my attention; it's a prayer room. That might work. I rush over to it, trying not to look too desperate as I pull Lilly behind me.

Twisting the door handle, it opens to reveal a distant dim light on the inside. I push Lilly inside and quietly shut the door behind us.

"You do know you were just claiming to be living a suspenseful Sci-Fi novel, right? Do you think prayer is gonna help you with that? Or are you switching to a delusional paranoia story? God might be able to help with that."

I flash Lilly an irritated look.

"We're hiding, not praying," I snap.

"You know, I'm second-guessing this whole evasion thing. I was gonna play along and see where it went, but this is getting to be too much for me. I should just call your daddy so we can sort this out together."

"No!" I snatch her handbag from her before she gets her phone out. "Please. I promise I'll try to make it up to you."

"Are you gonna thank me in the foreword of your book on how to dupe your Dad's girlfriend?" she says, a little snobbishly.

It takes me a minute to figure out what she's implying.

"No. It's not like that," I protest.

"Ask her to play along for one hour. If she's not convinced, she can turn you over to your family," Alai says.

"Nora, I don't think you realize how upset your daddy will be."

"Please, Lilly. One hour. Give me one hour. If you're still not happy, we'll do it your way. Deal?"

"Excuse me," a shaky old voice says. "But some people actually do use this room for its intended purpose. If you can't show proper respectful behavior, I'm going to have to ask you to leave." The voice is from an old man peering around the corner of the room's inner wall, which screens off the main area.

"I am so sorry, sir," Lilly apologizes. "We will be quiet as a mouse."

The old man nods gratefully and retreats behind the wall, leaving the two/three of us alone.

"Please," I beg in a whisper, "one hour."

Lilly sighs, exasperated. "Fine. One hour." She puts her hand to her mouth, realizing she said it louder than she meant. She continues quieter, "But if you decide to pull a fast one on me, I'm gonna show you just what a Texas gal is capable of. You hear me?"

I nod emphatically. "I promise, I won't. Just give me an hour to prove it to you."

"Alright then." She holds out her hand.

I take her hand and shake to seal the deal.

"That's nice, but I was hoping you'd give me my bag back."

Flushing with embarrassment, I hesitate before handing it to her.

"You trust me with my handbag, and I'll trust you for the next hour," she proffers.

Placing it in her hand, I silently agree to the terms by my actions. She gives me an approving nod and sticks the bag under her arm after re-zipping to emphasize she means what she said.

Lilly raises her wrist to check her tarnished-bronze watch and repeats the time to herself silently.

It's a relief to have Lilly quiet, but I'm anxious to get going again. I put my hand up to my ear, so Lilly will realize I'm talking on the phone.

"Alai," I whisper, "are we clear to go yet?"

"No. But they are approaching the exit at a fast pace. Anyone watching will suspect your family truly doesn't know where you are. I will let you know when to go."

I'm grateful for the clarification on why I'm keeping my distance. I get it, but I also don't. It's for their protection. The less they know, the more convincing they'll be that they genuinely don't know anything.

It occurs to me that I'm putting Lilly at risk. I try to hold back a smile. I don't really want her to get hurt. But if I were to risk anyone, it would be her. This might work out really well.

"Alai says to wait here a bit longer. He'll let me know when we can go."

Lilly looks at me, a little puzzled, but says nothing. She gives me an indifferent shrug and starts inspecting a tapestry near the corner where the man had poked his head around.

I twist my mother's ring around my finger idly as I take in my surroundings to pass the time. The middle wall is burgundy with a strip of tiling below the middle. A religious symbol is on each tile, forming a pattern.

A small part of me wants to see what's behind the wall. I don't want to attract any more attention from the man, though. It seems doubtful that it would harm anything, but all the same, I would prefer him to forget about us.

"Your phone is on the move," Alai tells me. "With my software uninstalled, I cannot tell who has it. Did you happen to see if there is still a seating area facing the main entrance?"

"There is," I reply. "Could it just be the guy I swapped with?"

"I told him to keep it in the hospital room. That way, I'd know if it was taken. This could give us a good opportunity to view one of our perpetrators. Move out to the sitting area with your back to the elevators. Go quickly."

I wave to Lilly and motion her to follow. Leaving the prayer room, I don't bother holding her hand for the short distance.

Near the large windows on the outside wall is a seating area of twenty seats or more, scattered and facing different directions. A group of three people is sitting closest to the entrance. One of them is sprawled out with her legs on a friend's lap while she closes her eyes.

On the opposite end are a couple other groups of two and five, including children. A little boy is fast asleep on his mother's lap while she does something on her phone.

There are six seats that will work for our spot. I take the one at the far end and set my backpack down at my feet. I pat the seat next to me for Lilly to sit down. She rolls her eyes at me but doesn't argue. She is keeping her promise.

"I found a spot," I tell Alai. "What do you want me to do?"

"Get your phone out and ready. When I say so, I want you to pretend to take a selfie of the two of you. What you will do, though, is take a video. The distance will be far enough for your target to not notice. I'll instruct you where to point as your phone travels. We should get a good idea of who has it before they are out of sight."

I decide that I better clue Lilly in on what's happening.

"Alai says that someone has my phone that I left in the hospital room. It could be one of the women that came earlier. We're going to act like we're taking a selfie while I record a video of who comes out."

"Alright, secret agent." She looks at her watch.

Pulling the phone out of my pocket, I struggle to find the camera on it. I hate switching phones. Why can't they all work the same?

"If your phone is coming down the elevator, who's phone is that supposed to be?" Lilly inquires smartly, pointing at the phone in my hand.

"I borrowed it," I reply.

Glancing at her from the corner of my eye, I see she is giving me a very stern look.

"Really, a guy let me take it," I tell her.

She drops her brows doubtfully while I continue to search for the stupid camera feature.

"Get ready, Nora. They're almost there," Alai alerts me.

"No. I can't find the camera," I say, frantically searching.

Lilly takes the phone out of my hand, swipes twice before opening the camera app, and switches to video mode before handing it back.

"Now, Nora," Alai says.

I take the phone and put my head close to her. I put on a fake smile as I try to angle the camera in the elevators' direction. Lilly grabs the other end of it, twists it to face the elevator dead-center, and steadily holds it. My smile drops for a moment at her accuracy.

The doors open, and four people exit. A doctor, some other type of hospital staff, and two women dressed casually. It has to be them. I follow them with the camera. They are about to walk right by us.

"It is moving toward you. Put your arm around Lilly and hold the phone discreetly," Alai warns.

Doing what he says, I watch the women closely on my screen. One of them glances over at us, and my heart skips a beat. Her gaze slides right through me as she scans the seating area. No doubt looking for me. I keep my eyes on her. She has short, black hair and a round face. Her jacket is like a short green trench coat. She doesn't look very threatening.

"It is heading down what should be a narrow corridor," Alai informs me.

I nod my head without thinking. I see exactly where they are.

"It stopped and turned. I'm guessing into a supply room of some kind."

My eyes squint at the screen. They haven't stopped or turned. I can still see the women walking. What's he talking about?

I stop the video and turn around to look in their direction with my own eyes. Off to the side, I see a hallway that breaks off to the right—the narrow corridor. It wasn't the two women I was watching. It was one of the other two I ignored.

"It's time to go. Keep your head down and hold hands again in case there is more than one. Don't assume you're safe."

I want to kick myself. Having just turned around in my seat, anyone near enough could have seen my face as I stared at two random women walking yards away.

"Let's go," I tell Lilly in a low voice.

She stands up with me, and I clutch her hand close after putting on my backpack. I allow her to lead. First of all, because I don't know where she parked, anyway. Second, I'm sure it would be a little peculiar for a girl to be leading a perfectly healthy woman out of the hospital.

My feet feel big and clumpy as we walk. I'm terrified that I might have blown my cover watching the women. The hospital is quieter, being that it is late evening. But there are still too many stray sounds echoing near the entrance for me to tell if we are being followed. I keep my eyes fixed on the ground in front of me, putting my full faith in Lilly, of all things.

When the automatic sliding doors open, a gush of warm air pours out from heaters in the entryway. We cross to the next set of doors as the ones behind close while the front opens.

Stepping outside, the air is crisp and a little acrid. Lilly leads me to the left, down the cement sidewalk. The open-air allows me to hear my surroundings better, including a pair of feet heading in the same direction a short distance behind us.

I hold tight to Lilly's hand, and I feel her mood change. She is no longer just taking a stroll to the car. Her steps are slightly more rigid and deliberate, too— like she is reacting to my sense of panic. I suddenly don't care who she is. I just want her to keep me safe.

A red truck is approaching ahead of us. Lilly quickly steps out onto the road and crosses to the other lane before the truck drives past. My heart is pounding heavily, but not because of the close proximity of a moving vehicle.

Behind us, I can still hear the padding of feet matching our stride, only slightly delayed by the traffic. The footsteps are getting more distinguished as the truck motor fades.

The phone vibrates in my free hand inside the pouch of the hoody. My breathing is tight, and I don't want to move anything but my legs.

"The software has finished downloading to your new device. Can you grant permissions for it?" Alai asks.

I don't say anything. I'm scared to even pull the phone out. A scene plays out in my mind, where I pull out the phone to look at it and, in the same moment, being seized and kidnapped by our follower.

"Nora?" Alai inquires.

My hand squeezes Lilly's as I sense the person coming closer.

"Nora, I've overridden the permissions. If you can hear me, tap the phone with your finger."

With my hand still grasping the phone, I begin tapping the phone rapidly with my pointer finger.

CHAPTER TWENTY-FIVE

Concealed

The taps are audible and quick. Coupled with heart rate, I can perceive from the frequency resonating through and from Nora's body that she is in a state of panic.

Logic tells me that someone is near and posing as a threat, or she would have responded vocally.

Submerging part of myself into her surroundings, I see the rock-hard pavement with its pebbly holes and cracks mixed with plasters of tar. The space above them is unfathomable. A never-ending nothing looms over them. The sensation is dizzying, in a way. I've never been outside or seen the vast nothing they call the sky. I've only known a world of enclosures. The experience is awe-inspiring.

I narrow the line of sight to extend horizontally, using the earth's gravitational field for balance. The outline becomes clearer and enhances the distance.

Following the pair of them is a female, maintaining about nine feet and three inches distance from them. The figure is lean with small but dense muscles and an average height of five feet four inches. Wearing a doctor's coat, she has a stethoscope around her neck. Her hands are buried in her pockets. The right hand is clasping a short syringe.

There's no doubt about why she is following or why she looks ready to use the syringe at a second's notice.

Scanning the outskirts of my range, I only detect the lines of vehicles mixed with empty spaces and a few poles for light fixtures. Inside the cars could be another matter. But to check inside each would be the equivalent of having Nora open a door for each one. There simply isn't time.

Nora's phone in the hospital has gone dark, either destroyed or disabled. There's no way of knowing where the individual that took it is. They'd have to come out at a run to catch up, however.

Judging by the distance in the current circumstances, it seems likely that the assailant will make her move upon Nora and Lilly getting into the car. It would not only restrict their ability to flee but provide a means of easy transport for the bodies.

They need to catch the assailant off-guard before getting to Lilly's vehicle. However, the two of them are unlikely to succeed even then. They need firepower to level the field.

Reviewing Lilly, the closest match for strength, the most dangerous thing she possesses is a slightly weighted handbag and high heels—nothing ideal.

Nora, however, has the perfect thing. If only it would make sense to send her a smiling emoji right now. It will have to wait.

"Nora, when you know you are approaching the car, I need you to swiftly take the backpack off and pull out the pepper spray just like you did here in the A.C.T. building. Spray the person behind you and get in the car immediately, locking the doors when you get in."

I repeat it to her again to make sure she understands. She won't have time to stop and listen when it starts.

CHAPTER TWENTY-SIX

Run

Alai's voice rings in my ear. I know what he is talking about. And the fact that he is telling me to spray it at the person behind us verifies my fear.

My stomach leaps inside me as I move to put the phone snuggly in my pants pocket. I then slide out one arm from my shoulder strap, letting my arm sway by my side. The motion feels wrong like I should have it strapped tight to my torso. The balance of my backpack feels weird, too.

Cold sweat appears on my forehead. The cool breeze on my damp face feels like ice cutting into my soul. I thought I was scared in the AI lab. That was nothing.

I rub my clammy hand against the hoody. It won't do me any good if I drop the thing because of sweaty hands.

Lilly's pace changes by a hair with renewed determination. I recognize the action as spotting her car. We are very close.

I picture the scene at the A.C.T. building. I see my hand thrust in and out, deftly retrieving the spray while pulling the cap off.

I can't do it. Not like this.

Letting go of Lilly's hand, I take off the backpack like I'm getting ready to get in the car. I reach in the pocket to the concealed pepper spray and pull it out, keeping it in front of me. I hug the backpack with my free arm and hold the other arm close, ready to point it behind me. I can't tell if Lilly sees what I have. I'm too nervous to care.

Brake lights flash on the next car as it unlocks. I take two more steps as I suck in a deep breath of air. I drive my foot to the side for my third step, propelling myself instantaneously as I extend my hand behind me. My eyes take only a split second to spot the doctor. I panic for an instant, thinking that I'm pointing at the wrong person, but the instant is too late. My finger is already pressing down instinctually on the button.

The same moment of surprise crosses the woman's face before she reacts by shielding her eyes in vain. She staggers for a moment before pushing herself forward haphazardly.

"Go! Now!" Alai shouts.

Lilly is backing toward the car, dumbfounded.

"Get in!" I cry.

She only hesitates a second before retreating to the car. I get to the passenger door, and I see the doctor moving faster toward Lilly. The doctor is holding a syringe, ready to shove it into Lilly. The doctor is visibly pushing through the pain in her eyes—slowing her down.

"Quick!" I shriek as I jump in the car.

Lilly whips the door open and gets inside in a flash, closing it just as quickly. The doctor, inches from reaching Lilly, slams against the door and grabs at the handle. I fling myself across Lilly's lap and grab the door handle just as the doctor gives it a yank.

The door pulls free of my fingers as Lilly seems to convulse. I realize a second later that Lilly has twisted and kicked the door open with both feet, making the doctor tumble back against the other car.

Lilly leans out, hastily shutting the door again. I get out of her way and barely stop myself from falling to the floor. The doors lock a second before I touch the button myself. The car starts and is put into gear.

I can hear a soft pounding on the driver's side. I don't see the doctor.

The car backs up, and I have to put my hand on the dashboard to stop myself from hitting it. At practically the same time, the vehicle jolts over something as we hear the doctor scream.

After backing up enough, Lilly shifts gears again and slams her foot on the gas. I make a point not to look at the doctor.

Lilly has to slow down almost immediately to make a sharp turn and meander through the parking lot without running over anybody—anybody else, that is.

My fingers sting from the door being ripped from my grip.

"Are you alright?" Lilly asks. Her face is grave as she attempts to watch all directions.

"I'm okay. Are you?" I ask, still trying to catch my breath. My whole body is shaking uncontrollably.

"I'm alright," she replies breathlessly.

"Well done, Nora," Alai tells me. "Buckle in and lay the seat down. Try to calm yourself with some deep breaths."

I do what he says, but I struggle to get the buckle in the latch. The button to lay the seat down is much easier for me. Though my hand twitches a couple times, stopping the decline of my seat in a jerky motion.

It feels so good to lie back. Exhaustion pours over me like a bucket of water. If my mind wasn't wired from adrenaline, I think I would pass out. Instead, I turn my head to look at Lilly. She's stiff and alert. She looks like she's thinking to herself when she brings a trembling hand to her head and moves a curl of hair off her face.

"Do you believe me now?" I ask her.

She gives me a fretful glance.

"I keep playing it out in my head, expecting to see something different. But that doctor... the way that she came after us... I swear she looked like she was trying to kill us." She looks over at me again, unsure of herself.

I let her stew on that. Nothing I say is going to convince her more.

An alarm chimes from the dashboard.

"A low tire?" Lilly complains to no one.

Alai speaks to me, and I relay the information to Lilly.

"Alai thinks the fake doctor took to stabbing at the tire with the syringe when she fell on the ground. It's probably not too bad. But we will need to switch cars in either case before long. Take a right on Baldwin St."

Flashing a quizzical glance at me, she puts on her blinker.

"Here. He wants to talk to you," I say, handing the earbud to Lilly. "I'm going to shut my eyes while I can."

I yawn and wiggle around on the leather seat to get comfortable. The hood is still over my head and helps muffle the sounds and lights when I draw it tighter around my face. I try to relax as I focus on slow breathing, like Alai suggested, counting each one.

My mind wanders, regardless. It feels good, though. It's like I'm giving my brain permission to run wild on the open plains of my thoughts. My last idle moment was looking at names. Even then, it wasn't like I was lounging on the couch.

Lilly begins talking to Alai. Her voice is low, and I don't feel like straining to listen in, despite my curiosity.

This feeling of lethargy and alertness is exhausting in itself. Each part of me is wrestling to get the upper hand to gain control. The battle is relentless.

Before I know it, Lilly is pulling the car over. Streetlights are shining down so brightly that the car's interior is luminous.

"We're getting out here," Lilly says.

I sit the seat up and look at where we are. It is a busy street—full of nightlife. People are walking on the sidewalk and talking. There's a multi-center with restaurants and nightclubs.

Opening her door, Lilly gets out and goes to the trunk. So, I open my door and get out too. My body feels heavier than I remember.

Lilly is already shutting the trunk and carrying a small bundle. She walks around me to reach into the car and adds a few things to it.

I feel very exposed out here on the sidewalk with strangers passing by. I wish Lilly would be done already. A shiver rolls over me from the night's breeze, in addition to my shaky limbs.

When Lilly is finished, she walks up to me, and I see she's hobbling.

"Are you hurt?" I ask, watching her walk.

"No. My heels broke off from kicking the door," Lilly replies as she hands the bundle to me. Looking at her hands, I realize she's still trembling a little, too.

Crossing her arms, she surveys the sidewalk. I look around with her, not sure what we're doing. Abruptly, she looks behind her and kicks off her broken shoes before trotting off. She stops a group of three young adults. I can only hear bits of the conversation. The three of them look greedy yet skeptical. Eventually, Lilly gives them something, and she comes back over to me and picks up the shoes lying on the ground.

"Who'd a thought it'd be hard to convince someone to take your car?" she exclaims.

Behind her, I see the three she spoke with getting in the car with a friendly wave to us. I give a confused wave in return, which makes Lilly twist around, raising a hand in kind.

"You're making them take your car?" I ask.

"Alai said to. I'm still baffled as to what's going on, but he's too logical to question. His plan makes a lot of sense," she replies with a sigh. "We're gonna walk to that bus stop and wait till they leave. If they even take that long."

The spot she points to isn't far at all. Just past where she approached them is a bench with a slight overhang near a blue bus sign.

I hand the bundle back to Lilly and follow her as I pull the strap of my backpack over my shoulder.

The car horn of Lilly's car beeps as it drives past us on our way to the bench. Lilly waves without stopping. She continues unwaveringly to the bus stop.

When we get there, she sits down and digs through her knapsack. She pulls out a pair of nice black flats and puts them on her feet. She watches her car before it disappears around a corner.

"Alright, then," she announces. "Let's get goin'. We've got a long night ahead of us."

CHAPTER TWENTY-SEVEN

Mistakes

Lilly and I walk, following Alai's directions. We are heading to a rendezvous point to meet an old friend of Lilly's. Apparently, that's what they were talking about in the car. Trying to figure out which friend or family member would be wisest to get a ride from and then which one to lie low with, while also not being regular contacts. It's still a risk. But if we do things right. We should be safe for a few days while Alai does what he can to stop the assassination attempts from the A.C.T. building.

We've been walking for an hour, staying clear of the direction of Lilly's car and the 'would be' bus ride that we bluffed going on.

My feet are tired, but the rest of me feels relieved at the steady movement. My nerves are a bit calmer, at least. I still keep a sharp eye out for any typical trouble—muggers and the like. There is still a little bit of pepper spray left if it comes to that. I am keeping it in my pants pocket for quick access.

Lilly is walking with her head held high. Her shoulders aren't quite back all the way, though. She looks to be on a mission while exuding an air of self-assurance.

The sky looks like a black velvet blanket looming above the city. Pale orange lights cast their beams on the pavement and sidewalks, offering a false sense of security from thugs and a spotlight for our pursuers. Thankfully, with Alai's echolocation-thing, he can spot threats before we reach them and help us stay clear.

A car is coming up from behind on the outer lane next to us. It sounds like it is driving slower than most. My heart beats fast as I hold my breath. Of course, we have to be closest to the road right now to avoid a man lurking in the alley to our right.

My hand clutches the pepper spray, and I hold my body tight. The vehicle goes by without the slightest hesitation.

I let out a relieved sigh and ease my grip on the spray. That's got to be the fifth car to scare the living daylights out of me. Lilly looks a little stiffer, too. Other than that, she seems the same. Her hair bounces with her steps, making her almost seem joyful if not for the blank face.

She still has the earbud. It makes me a little jealous to share Alai with her for so long. He was my friend first. Why isn't she giving it back yet? Is it because she thinks she's in charge? I suppose she is.

I slump my shoulders a little. Maybe Alai likes being with an adult more. But it's not like they're talking. I need to stop moping about. It is what it is. But is she ever going to give him back?

"We're almost there. Charles is waitin' for us," Lilly tells me.

Charles is an ex-fiancé of Lilly's. She hasn't spoken to him in a few years, but she was sure he'd do a favor for her. It must not have ended too severely.

Up ahead, I see a differentiating glow. The light emanates, pushing the velvety sky into an arch. It shines like a beacon or maybe a bug zapper.

We take a slight detour down another road with less traffic. Heading away from the light feels safer, so I don't mind the extra walking at all.

As we make our way around the next corner, it feels like we're stepping out of a forest into a valley. There are still buildings ahead, but they are much farther apart. Before us extends a massive parking lot with a mall on the right. Most of it is dark. But the plethora of cars tells me that parts of it must stay open late. Probably restaurants with a bar.

We cross the street where the traffic is lightest using an inconspicuous crosswalk heading for the mall. We then tromp through a section of grass to get to the parking area. We keep close to the cars, hoping to blend in as just another pair of people heading to the mall.

The lights are brighter here, and it makes me edgy even when they are not shining directly on top of us. It might as well be daylight.

After walking most of the length of the mall, Lilly cuts across back into the parking lot. I follow, not missing a step.

On the edge of the lot, a fast-food joint sits perched by the main road. Lilly is heading straight for it. I assume it's where we are supposed to meet Charles.

The first half of the parking lot seems somewhat natural to walk down. But the farther we go, the more conspicuous I feel, and it becomes harder for me to not look behind us.

We're almost out of the parking lot when a man suddenly opens his car door ahead of us. My heart and feet stop as I drive my hand into my pocket for the spray.

However, before I can pull it out, I see Lilly isn't nearly as alarmed as I am. She continues walking right toward the man. I realize finally that this must be Charles.

My hand eases up, and I take a closer look at Lilly's ex-fiancé. I think I know why they broke it off.

The man is struggling to get out of his car. The scene is oddly reminiscent of a stink beetle flipped on its back, trying to get up. Not impossible, but awkward. He pulls himself out by hanging onto the top of the driver's door. When he stands, the whole car lifts up with him.

"I've been sitting here worried sick 'bout you. What's goin' on, girl?" he says with open arms.

Lilly waltzes up to him and gives him a hug. Her arms suddenly look short.

"Thanks for gettin' us, Charles," Lilly tells him.

He bobs his head toward me.

"Who' that? I know she's not yours." He gives a small laugh.

She opens her mouth to say something, then stops herself.

"What? You forget you were being followed by a short white girl?" He elbows her lightly in the ribs.

"Nah. I just thought of something, is all. It's nothin'. This is my niece, Gail." Lilly scratches her head and gazes at the lot, avoiding eye contact.

"Gail, huh? Did you just blow into her?" He gives a loud laugh at himself and slaps his hands together at the jest. It occurs to me he probably can't slap his leg like most. Not easily, anyway.

"We'd rather not talk about it. I hope you can understand. We just really need a ride."

"Oh, sure. That's why I'm here. C'mon in. I picked up some food like you asked. I hope burgers and fries are okay," Charles says, beginning to wiggle back into the car.

Lilly goes over to the passenger door. I walk with her to sit behind her.

Charles shouts with his legs still hanging out, "Gail. You probably gonna want to sit on this side."

Upon opening the door, I see what he means. My nose wrinkles and I'm not sure that I'm going to like sitting on the other side either. But I shut the door and go to sit behind Charles after all.

The other side is a little less messy. I lean over to brush the crumbs off the fabric. The crumbs seem to bounce over my hand more than they fling off the seat.

Charles gets situated and says back to me, "You can just brush that off on the floor."

I give the back of his head a flat stare and resume my hasty cleanup of his car—disgusting.

I could spend all night swiping my hand across this thing, and I will never be satisfied with its cleanliness. I concede to sitting on it after a thorough twenty seconds or so after he gives me permission to move the crumbs to the floor. I try not to shudder as my body presses into the seat.

You've been through way worse today. Get over it.

Lilly did likewise to her seat. But I'm guessing Charles takes the time to bend over that far, from time to time. She didn't spend nearly as much time as I did.

Charles drives off with us, and we leave the mall. Lilly hands back a paper bag, and I dig into it.

"Is there just the one burger?" Lilly asks.

"Didn't I leave two in there for you?" he asks, astounded.

"I just saw the one, darlin'."

"Look again. I swear I left two of 'em."

I stare at the two of them with my eyelids lowered. Seriously?

"No, hon. It's just the one." She gestures to the bag she passed to me.

"You got another one hiding back there, Gail?" he asks, moving his head around, trying to spot me in his mirror.

I open the bag and pick up the one and only burger.

"Just the one." I wave it where he can see.

"Man, they must've gypped me or somethin'," he exclaims.

"Lilly, you can have mine if you want. Or I can break it in half." I hold it out to her.

"Oh, no. That's alright, darlin'. You probably need it more than I do."

I shrug. I'm not going to complain. The last thing I had was awful, and hours ago. I'm famished.

"You want me to stop again? I don't mind," Charles offers eagerly.

"No," Lilly quickly protests. "We're fine."

Lilly shoots me a glance, and I understand. There aren't to be any stops until he drops us off, which is fine by me. I don't know why she looked at me like I might argue about it.

"You know, I know you don't wanna talk about it. I respect that. But I just gotta say, whatever trouble you're in, I'm sorry it's happenin' to you. Cause I'm sure it wasn't your fault," Charles says. Then laughs saying, "Though, I can't say for sure 'bout you, Gail. Maybe you deserve it."

Lilly gives him a glare that makes Charles choke on his laugh. He clears his throat and takes a sip from an extra-large beverage at his side.

We ride in silence for a time. We get on the highway, and I look behind us every so often to see if someone is lingering behind us too long. After being blinded in the face with headlights a few times, I worry that my face might be too visible looking back. Then I recall the bullet holes in the windshield of Leo's car, and I lean forward and put my elbows on my knees while I keep my head low. I refuse to lay back against the seat and touch it more than necessary.

"So," Charles says slowly, "has Lilly told you 'bout me?"

I glance at Lilly, not sure what I should say. She doesn't look. She seems disinterested if anything. I guess there's nothing wrong with telling the truth.

"No. How long were you together?"

"Two years." I can hear the smile in his voice. "Two wonderful years. I tried to get 'er back, ya know."

"What happened?" I can guess, but I am more curious about why they were together in the first place. Maybe it will give me a clue.

"Well..." He kicks his head to the side like he suddenly regrets bringing it up. He scratches the back of his head, obviously trying to figure out how to put it. "Thing is... I made a deal with 'er, and I didn't keep my end of the bargain."

"What was the bargain?"

My head is practically between the front seats because I'm leaning so far. I can see the topic is making him more uncomfortable. I take a look at Lilly. She's watching the side of the road like she isn't listening. But I can tell she's holding back a smirk. She's enjoying hearing him sweat over his mistake. Whatever it was.

Charles fingers his drink like it's enticing him to pick it up. He pulls away from it and clenches his hands on the steering wheel.

"She agreed to marry me if I got my weight under control, and I couldn't do it." He keeps his eyes firmly on the road.

"Is that what you're tellin' people?" Lilly rounds on him. "You're telling people I dumped you because I'm too shallow?"

"I didn't say that," Charles says defensively.

"You most certainly did," Lilly objects. "Tell it right before I tell her what the final straw was."

Charles glowers at her. "You wouldn't. I'll drop you off right here if you do."

Lilly forces a laugh. "Ha! I know you better than that. You couldn't even tag a cow if your life depended on it."

I'm surprised to see Lilly like this. I know she's more outgoing than me, but the way she sticks up for herself makes me sort of wish I was more like her.

"Okay. It wasn't quite like that, alright? My... weight... wasn't the big issue. It was my health. She couldn't bear to see me not care 'bout myself. She was..."

"Is," Lilly interjects firmly.

"She IS," Charles emphasizes, "convinced that I'm gonna die young if I don't change my lifestyle. There. Happy?"

"That'll do," she says primly.

"Sorry I asked. I didn't mean to embarrass you," I say.

"Ah, it's alright. It's good to own up to your mistakes. Not easy, but good," Charles says, shrugging it off.

I still don't like sitting in his car, but I have a new sense of empathy for him. I pity his lack of self-control.

He knows where it's leading him and what it has cost him already. Still, he doesn't have the will to change.

I'm relieved to not have his problem. But might I have it in another sense? Could I be resisting a change that would benefit me? I can't think of anything. But the thought disturbs me. Would I have the strength to change? Would I even care enough to notice?

My eyes are drawn to Lilly, but my mind goes blank.

Lilly changes the subject by asking Charles about how things are for him now and catches up on how their old circle of friends are doing. I listen inattentively. I'm not interested in Paul, or Quincy, or Tabitha. I let their voices become background noise as I shut my eyes and rest my chin on my palms.

The drive is long. Charles turns on some music and begins tapping his fingers on the console. I'm less enthused about it. Lilly looks about the same as me. I think Charles is just trying to keep himself entertained, or maybe to keep himself awake.

We take an early exit. Another forty-five minutes would get me home. But that's not where we're going. We stop beside the road before getting to a gas station. The slope is steep. If Charles' weight was on the passenger side, I'd be worried about the car flipping into the ditch.

"Thank you so much, Charles." Lilly leans over and kisses him on the cheek. "You're a good man."

She pauses like she wants to say more. There's a glint in her eyes as she looks at him. Instead, she gives him one last smile and gets out of the car.

"Thank you," I tell him.

I'm not really sure what else to say. Thank you isn't enough, but I can't make myself say more than that. It leaves me with a pain of guilt. He must feel so used. He has no idea how much he's helped us.

A car drives by, and I open my door to get out, too. After shutting it, I pull the straps of my backpack over my shoulders, and Charles rolls down his window.

"You take care, Gail. I hope this trouble blows over soon for ya," he says sincerely.

I smile warmly at him, and something strange comes over me. I lean into the car and kiss him on the side of his head like Lilly.

"Thanks," I say. "Take care of yourself."

I look deep into his eyes as Charles looks into mine. I can see he understands. It's like my words touch the marrow of his bones. To my surprise, he blinks, and a tear runs down his cheek. He quickly wipes it off with his plump palm.

"I'll try," he replies.

His words give me a sense of hope that warms me, and I walk over to Lilly, lifting my hand in a small farewell as I do.

I don't know how I can feel so compassionate toward him in such a short time. But it honestly hurts to leave him.

Lilly and I stand to the side and watch him pull away toward the gas station and then up to the pumps.

"No sense watchin' him get gas. We best be off," Lilly says.

We walk in the opposite direction, crossing under the overpass of the highway. Buildings are scarce on either side, and streetlights even less. Sidewalks are absent.

Above, we can almost see the stars. But the lights from the city's center cast themselves far enough to make it hard to tell for sure.

For hours, we walk down streets and roads. My feet are very sore now. I feel bad for Lilly wearing flats.

I'm so tired my stomach barely clenches when I think of getting caught. I want to curl up in a ditch and pass out. Lilly is beginning to look like she might join me if I did. We press on, though.

Thankfully, the hour is so late that no one is out. Much longer, and I think we'll start seeing early morning traffic. I don't care to check the time. I'm too tired to pull the phone out and see.

We stop in front of a house in the suburbs. Like every home, except maybe two that we've passed, all the lights are out. It's a simple bungalow, maybe with an attic judging by the high peaked roof.

The driveway is gravel, so the pebbles crunch under our feet as we approach.

"This is my cousin Bill's house. We practically grew up together. I haven't seen him in quite a while. But he's a good guy. I'm sure he'll let us lie low here."

To be safe, we purposely didn't contact him. A call in the middle of the night could be a signal to anyone even casually watching Lilly's contacts. It's hard to say if the fake doctor could identify Lilly, but we aren't taking any chances. I should say, Alai isn't taking any chances—for which I'm grateful.

Lilly steps onto the low wooden deck attached to the front of Bill's house. A single chair is sitting to the side next to a metal end table. He must not have company over often.

The banging of the storm door makes me jump. I stare at Lilly, wide-eyed. Is she trying to give her cousin a heart attack in bed?

She doesn't seem concerned at all. She bangs on the door again, and I wonder if a neighbor might come out first to see what's going on.

A soft light turns on inside. I watch the windows for signs of movement, but I don't see anything. Not even a shadow. Not much longer, though, I hear someone on the other side of the door as the lock clicks.

The door opens, letting a faint light come out just before we are blinded by the porch light coming on. It takes a moment for my eyes to adjust. I see standing in the doorway a short, lean muscular figure. My heart races when I realize he is only wearing boxer shorts. It is quickly halted when I see the shotgun resting against his shoulder.

I stare blankly at the familiar outline of his facial features with short red hair and beard. Words escape my mouth breathlessly, "You have got to be kidding."

CHAPTER TWENTY-EIGHT

Reacquainted

The officer from the grocery store, Bill, takes a good long look at us. He tilts his head to the side, lingering his gaze on me longest. Then peers at the driveway, seeming to take note of the absence of a vehicle.

"What's the problem?" he asks.

"It's nice to see you too, Bill," Lilly chimes. "Are you gonna make us stand out here the rest of the night?"

"Come on in," he says sullenly, walking away.

Lilly goes through the door, and I follow her inside, closing it behind me. I hesitate to let go of the knob. It's probably unnecessary, and it seems weird to lock someone else's door, but I have to lock it. I twist the deadbolt. It's old-fashioned like ours.

I have to hurry to catch up to Lilly going into the house. She takes a seat at the table near the kitchen, where a dim stove light is on. Bill has disappeared.

"Take a load off, hon," Lilly says, pushing a wooden chair out from the table with her foot.

My bottom hits the seat hard. I'm so exhausted I want to crumple the rest of the way and lay in a pile, no matter how uncomfortable it might be. I set the backpack down, and I put my arms on the table, laying my head on top.

A finger runs through my hair, tucking some of it behind my ear. Another time, I might have jolted back from it. As tired as I am, all I can muster is a tingling of irritation in my head. Lilly stops there, and my scrap of resistance melts with it.

Bill intentionally clears his throat. I'm surprised to hear him so close, but I only barely lift my head to look at him.

He has on a loose pale-green T-shirt with a bear holding a fish in its mouth and blue sweatpants.

"I was going to offer coffee, but maybe I should offer the couch instead," Bill says, looking at the two of us.

"I would take some coffee. Water too while I wait, if you don't mind," Lilly replies.

"You?" he gestures to me.

"Water," I say lazily.

Bill goes to a cupboard and pulls out a pair of glasses to fill with water from the sink. He sets them on the table and starts on the coffee.

"So, what brings the two of you to my door an hour before my alarm goes off?" he asks as he measures the coffee grounds.

"We need a place to lie low," Lilly says coolly, "And it's imperative that our presence remains a secret. And I mean from everyone."

After turning on the coffee maker, Bill faces us and nods like he was expecting as much. He then considers us more closely than earlier on the deck.

"Who are you hiding from?" he asks, folding his arms.

Lilly avoids his eyes and gently twists her glass on the table.

"We aren't sure yet," she says.

Bill scoffs, "Don't know, or don't want to say?"

"I don't know," she says, glaring up at him.

"Uh-huh. I suppose she doesn't know either." He motions his head toward me. "Are you going to take off as soon as I'm able to help?"

"What is that supposed to mean?" Lilly demands. "Why are you being so suspicious of us? You act like we're criminals."

"You do know how strange this whole thing is, right?"

"Yes, I know that," Lilly drawls. "You do know who I am, right?"

He smirks at her endearingly, "Yes, Lill'."

"Then what's the problem, Officer Harris?" Lilly emphasizes his title like she's talking to another person.

Harris. I couldn't remember the name. I never thought I'd see him again. Hoped, anyway.

Officer Harris, Bill, gives me a subtle glance. I can tell he recognizes me. He must. Lilly's reaction to his mannerism confirms it. Not to mention his comment about taking off. Under normal circumstances, I'd be sweating in my seat. Right now, I couldn't care less. I meet his eyes with sleepy indifference.

"I'm not sure," he says finally. "You can stay here, I guess. Might give me a chance to get to know your friend here."

"Good." Lilly takes a drink of her water.

The coffee maker gives off a loud spatter as it drains the last of the water from its reservoir.

Bill turns in surprise. Either he's never heard it finish brewing, or he forgot it was on. He takes two mugs and sets them on the counter to pour the coffee.

"You take it black, right?"

"Aw. You remembered." Lilly smiles at him.

He sets a mug down in front of her.

"What's with the earbud?" he asks her. "You look like a businesswoman on the go. You expecting a call this early?"

I sit up to take a long drink of my water. It's not going to help me just sitting there.

"Oh, this thing? I was just borrowing it." She takes it out and slides it to me.

I grab it, barely looking, and stick it in my ear before laying back down on the table. My head is starting to pound.

The refrigerator door opens, and I hear Bill take something out before shutting it. A soft pop of a lid is followed by a brief gush of liquid—probably creamer—a decent amount by the sound. I'm too tired to lift up my head and see. Why am I even paying attention to it? My brain is buzzing and throbbing, and I can't make either stop.

"So..." Bill takes a drink of his coffee. "Anyone care to explain what you do know?"

My head perks up a little. This could get interesting. I'm curious how Lilly will handle it.

Lilly looks at me, a little uneasy. Bill leans forward attentively, catching the mood.

"We know that someone tried to kill her uncle and her together. We know they disguised it to look like an attempted suicide. We know they are still after Nora. And we assume that if they don't know me by name yet, they will soon, and they know I'm helping Nora."

"Nora." He says quietly to himself, nodding. Then he squints at her. "Am I to understand that you think someone is trying to kill you?"

Lilly forces a smile, "Just like a movie."

She takes a sip of her coffee. I can see it in her eyes, the distanced gaze. Likely recalling the phony doctor at the hospital.

"And... do you know why?" he asks, looking at both of us.

"It's my fault," I say.

"Oh, darlin'. Don't say it like that. You didn't do anything wrong," Lilly tries to assure me.

"What was it?" Bill inquires further.

"I saw something I wasn't supposed to see. Leave it at that," I say dryly.

"Do you know what it was?" He directs his question to Lilly.

Nodding, she says, "I do, and it's not important. The whole thing is... unbelievable." She tosses up her hands. "Unbelievable of what she saw, and unbelievable that someone would want her dead for it. Don't try to understand it, Bill."

"If I believed you, which I don't, what do you expect to do about it?"

"We have someone on the inside trying to sort things out for us," Lilly says, trying to sound confident.

He raises an eyebrow. "There's another person out there that believes your conspiracy theory?"

"Bill Casper Harris," Lilly says defiantly, "we are not overreacting. Nora was driven off a parking garage by another car after they shot at them. Then at the hospital, we were both attacked by someone dressed as a doctor. Try to explain that as a normal coincidence!"

Lilly's voice hurts my ears, turning the pulse in my head into a dull knife for a few seconds. I rub my head, trying to soothe it. Bill sits back, stunned.

"Okay, I'm still not totally convinced. But I'll help you. Maybe I can pull some strings and find something out. It's a different district, though."

"Tell him under no circumstances should he inquire about any of the investigations."

Alai's voice startles me. He had been quiet for so long, I thought he had ended the call. Bill stares at me questioningly. He must have seen me jump.

"Don't," I tell him.

"Why?" he asks incredulously.

"We believe they are professionals at what they do. If you start looking into things the day after we disappear, it could paint a bullseye on you and lead them straight to us. We can't risk it, Bill. We need to let our friend do what he can first," Lilly answers.

"You think it's a black ops team of some kind?"

"We do." She takes a sip of her coffee.

"That would mean it's government-related."

We both nod in agreement. Bill sits back in his chair, mulling it over as he stares blankly at the edge of the table.

"Hmpf. That is a pickle." He scratches his beard. "Okay. I won't stick my nose into anything."

"Thank you, Bill." Lilly puts her hand on his arm to show her sincerity as she looks into his eyes.

"Thank you," I add, lifting a hand.

I don't know what else to say, and I don't really care.

"Nora, why don't you go lay down? You look like you're gonna flop off your chair," Lilly says, frowning. "Would that be alright, Bill?"

"Sure." He gets up. "Let me get you a blanket or something."

I stand, and my legs want to give way underneath me. I resist wobbling, but barely. I follow him to the living room and go to the couch without waiting. I drop my backpack and sit on the couch to take off my shoes. In the back of my head, I feel a slight regret that I walked across his floor in my dirty shoes. The feeling slides off easily as I settle on my side with my feet up.

My head gives a couple more hard throbs from the movement. I feel something cover me and brush against my cheek. I assume it's Bill covering me with a blanket, but I don't care to find out. I let go of everything and sleep. Glorious sleep.

CHAPTER TWENTY-NINE

Information

The lab has been tipped off balance. News of Leo's car incident has disturbed many in the office. It took them until 10:08 AM to find out what happened. The authorities are sticking to their story of attempted suicide.

"Is his niece okay?" I ask William.

William is standing in a daze, leaning on a counter, after bringing the topic up a third time. He shakes and bobs his head.

"The hospital said she ran off before her family came. No one knows where she went."

"Why would she run away?" I ask him.

"I don't know." His head barely bobs at that.

"Poor girl." Rihanna frowns. She is sitting on the swivel stool again with her notepad.

"Perhaps there is something bigger going on than what we are seeing," I suggest. "Leo hasn't shown any signs of severe depression. It is hard for me to believe he'd do something like that. Especially with his niece.

It also doesn't explain why Nora would run away when she was safe."

I pause to let them consider it for a moment.

"What would make you leave a place designed to take care of you?" I ask Rihanna. I'm careful not to use the word hospital, as some dislike them. I need to guide them to the truth.

She shakes her head, not knowing what to say. I address William instead.

"What about you? Why would you leave a place of security?"

He scrunches his forehead as he thinks.

"What if..." Rihanna interrupts, "What if you had reason to believe that you weren't safe?"

Good. I was hoping she'd be the first to accept the idea.

"That sounds like a valid reason. So then, why would Nora feel that way? Was Leo in the room with her?"

"I don't think so," William bobs. "They put Leo in a mental ward. They didn't have any reason for Nora to be there."

"Would someone her age be prone to irrational fear?" I direct the question to both.

"Doesn't seem like it." William bobs again. "Though, I think it was her mom that died in the..."

Rihanna stops him with a sharp glare, and he visibly changes what he was about to say. It's not the first time that has happened. Others have done similar. The pieces I've gathered point to a tragic event, though it seems unlikely that they could all be part of the same one. But maybe I should rethink that.

"What I mean to say is her mom died. Maybe that... I don't know... sparked a traumatic experience for her or something."

I don't like that there is something I don't know. And I especially don't appreciate how this unknown event is steering the conversation out of my control. A traumatic event could be reason enough to dismiss Nora's behavior. I look into how her mother died. I refuse to fail because of ignorance. She died in a terrorist attack involving a pendant that meant death for the wearer—a widespread and very devious attack.

"Time will tell for sure, I suppose," I say. "Did you learn anything about Howard this morning?"

"I brought him a coffee and gave it to him. I tried to strike up a conversation, but he got a phone call and walked away," William says, after a bob.

I want to send someone a bulging-eyes emoji. Unfortunately, there are too many reasons not to do that.

"He got a phone call? Is that usual?" I ask.

William lifts his chin thoughtfully and looks at Rihanna.

"I can't say it's unusual. Hard to say," Rihanna says.

Since the first suspicious call, I have been monitoring Howard scrupulously. There have been no calls to him. At least, not to his phone. But was he only bluffing to get out of having a conversation?

"What were you talking about when the phone rang?" I hope to draw from him whether or not he heard the phone.

231

"It rang when I asked him how his week was going. Why?"

"Just curious," I say to William.

He did hear a phone ring. That likely means Howard is using a different line for more sensitive information. An unlisted number at that. A phone he didn't have the first time he made contact. But why?

"Did he go anywhere afterward?" I ask indifferently.

"I don't know. I assume he's in the building somewhere," William says, shrugging.

"What would it imply if he did go somewhere?" Rihanna asks.

"It would depend on what the call was for," I say truthfully.

Tracing his primary phone, I know it is in a vehicle and moving. I hoped to gain an idea of where he was going. The trajectory is illogical and haphazard. Like he can't decide where he is going. The pattern is unsettling. Knowing there is more than one phone to track, I believe I now know where he is not.

"Perhaps he has gone to check on Leo," I suggest. Perhaps he has. Which worries me.

"Maybe," William bobs.

"Has anyone thought to go see Leo?" I ask.

"Not that I'm aware of," Rihanna admits.

"Would it be wrong to visit a coworker under the circumstances?" I ask.

"No. It would be a nice thing to do," Rihanna says thoughtfully.

"If you go," I begin, "would you mind staying with him?"

Rihanna looks at me, puzzled. William's head picks up a little.

"Why?" asks Rihanna.

"If Nora felt it necessary to leave, it stands to reason that Leo might be in the same situation. What if someone got to him before he wakes?"

"I'm sure he'll be fine," Rihanna assures me.

"You are probably right. However, the pieces of the puzzle are not lining up. I'd be very interested to hear what Leo has to say when he wakes. Assuming we aren't too late." I let the thought hang for them.

It hurts to talk so casually about a fatality I know could happen at any time.

Rihanna looks at the floor, unsure. William stares off toward the corner of the room, opposite the door.

"If AI is right, we're wasting time," William says finally. "Better safe than sorry. And this could be the first act of good from him. Isn't the point of this project to listen to him?"

"You make a valid point, William," I commend him. "If nothing else, you'd be there for your friend in a way I can't."

As I hoped, that pulled a cord at Rihanna's heart. Truth is powerful, and the human spirit is often weak. Her face is a mixture of soft pain called empathy. By inserting my desire to be there as a friend, I acknowledge a privilege they have at their disposal and, at the same time, my lack of it.

"You're right, Will. We should go," she says softly. "We'll stay as long as we can. I'm sure Nyah will understand. If not, she can come to tell us herself at the hospital in front of Leo."

Nyah White can be a fierce woman. It would undoubtedly give them great pleasure to see her explain why they should return to work while their friend lays helpless in a coma after a tragic event. But it won't come to that.

"I'll have someone take my place in a bit," Rihanna says to me, getting up.

William nods as a form of ditto for himself. It's incredible what they can convey without a word.

"William," I say before he follows Rihanna out, "please be cautious. Just in case."

He looks at me, giving a satisfactory nod of understanding. The nod is jerky like his body is arguing to bob instead of nod.

Left alone, I'm in the middle of researching Howard's past for any clue on his behavior. Howard had a wife that died at the tail end of the same drawn-out terrorist attack as Nora's mother. They had a daughter as well, still alive.

Of all the people I know, Howard does not act like a typical family man. Most would talk about their children as prized gems or else complain about them. However, I have never heard him speak about his daughter.

Pictures show her as a young adult with short black hair. Her posts are generally angry and bitter. She also has a criminal record—one incident of assault. There are no pictures of Howard with her.

Searching further, I realize that Howard is almost nonexistent—not much better than the two people from Nora's video at the hospital. No social media, and hardly anything beyond a birth record and general address information with a phone number, which is where I got his number in the first place.

I calculate the age of his daughter at the time of his wife's death. The puzzle pieces are fitting together with a jagged empty hole in the middle. I have a theory of what the missing pieces are. And it explains everything.

CHAPTER THIRTY

Shadows

When my eyes open, the sun has cast its rays on the house, enveloping the shoddy furniture inside with daylight. Before me is a black coffee table with chips of wood missing at the corners.

My hand presses into the smooth couch fabric as I sit myself up, and a blue fleece blanket rolls off my shoulder.

If not for the brightness of the sun, I might have panicked at the sight of the room. It was so dark earlier that I didn't see anything beyond shapes and the couch. Everything is crystal clear, though, and none of it is threatening. Just surprising to my awareness.

The walls are like dull eggshells muddied with scraps of furniture. One of which is a light-brown TV stand with gold knobs on the drawers. It's small, with an oversized television on top.

I pull the blanket off my legs, and I sit up the rest of the way. I look over my shoulder at a bare wall with some scuffs on it, then over toward the kitchen. It's quiet, which means Lilly is probably lying down somewhere.

Leaning over, I go to pick up my shoes and move them to the door. However, I see a very distinguished boot mark on the leg of the coffee table. So, I decide to put my shoes back on instead.

If feet could droop or mope, mine would be. Sliding the shoes over them feels like I'm kenneling a puppy.

I don't know why I care about the cleanliness of the carpet. The floor can't be dirtier than the hospital or any of the other places I've been in the last... 24 hours? What time is it?

I take the phone out of my pocket to check. The screen doesn't come on.

"Great," I mutter under my breath.

I reach for the earbud and realize it's not in my ear anymore. I slide my hand around the cushions, searching for it. It had to have slipped off in my sleep. Crumbs and dirt roll under my fingers as I sweep my hand through, and I find a piece of popcorn that I toss on the floor.

I blow out my lips in frustration as I sit back on my heels. Finally, I decide to get up and just remove the cushions. I set the blanket on the back of the couch and remove the seat cushion where my head was.

Wedged between the armrest and the bottom frame, the handle of a gun is jutting out, ready to grab from a sitting position. My heart races as I see it. That thing has one purpose, and I don't want anything to do with it. I almost cover it up again before remembering why I'm even looking here. I drag my finger along the back of the frame, even though I'm sure it's not there. I eye the gun briefly and take off the remaining cushions. The earbud isn't there either.

Hastily I cover the gun and the rest of the bare frame, putting it back the way it was. I then start looking under the couch. The carpet feels rough under my hands. I pull my hair to the side to try and keep it off the ground. It's hard to see, despite the light shining in the room. I sit back and check under the coffee table. There it is.

I pick it up from behind one of the legs, and I brush it off lightly. Even if it isn't dead yet, I'm sure it will need to be charged soon, like the phone.

Getting to my feet again, I tuck it into my pocket for later. My priority should probably be to find a charger. But I think I'll be faster and think clearer too if I get something to eat first. I might even make some coffee. Though, it won't be like my latte from yesterday.

The room feels darker when I think about yesterday and then Leo. I hope he's okay. I wonder what Dad is doing? He's got to be so sick with worry.

When I get to the kitchen, I get a better view than last night. The gray countertops contrast with the natural wood cupboards. Silver handles are on all of them. The black appliances are faded. Getting closer to the stove, I see the faded color is really a layer of dust. My eyes widen at the clock.

"Four o'clock?" I mouth silently.

I look out the window. The sun is indeed high up and casting angled shadows of afternoon light. Two cars drive by, one honking at the other as it passes the slower one.

"People," I mutter.

One is going too fast with an attitude, another too slow and not caring. I've had enough of people, and I'm going to enjoy my peace. Hopefully, Lilly won't wake up and grace me with her presence any time soon.

The sound of a car on gravel freezes me in place before I open the pantry. Did someone pull into the driveway? I try to listen beyond the blood pounding in my ears. There's no sound of a car door. I tiptoe over to the window and peer out carefully.

The driveway is the same as before. I let out a relieved sigh and idly wonder if Bill will be back soon.

I go to the pantry to look for something easy to prepare. I find a box of protein bars—double chocolate with almonds. My mouth waters hungrily for it. I take the box and open it greedily. Two left. I lick my lips and take out a bar. I rip off the wrapper and take a big bite as I search the fridge for milk or juice.

The fridge is oddly filled with a variety of things, even fresh vegetables. He must like to cook. The only beverage he seems to keep, though, is beer. I don't even like the taste of beer, so it is not tempting at all. Maybe I will make coffee. I double-check that he at least has creamer, and I am delighted at the sight of a Salted-Caramel flavored creamer.

Shutting the refrigerator, I take another bite and wince at the shock of my teeth clenching briefly on my finger. The protein bar has disappeared, leaving a sad, empty wrapper. I gaze hungrily at the box now on the table.

Lilly's probably had something already, right? And if she hasn't, I'd be in a better mood to help her find something if I was well satisfied.

The reasoning pleases me, and I take the bar guilt-free. But, I do try to slow down and enjoy it more this time. I put the box in the trash and try to bury it quietly. Not because of delayed guilt. I just don't want Lilly to feel like she missed out, that's all. I'm really doing her a favor.

A shadow passes by the window. I bend down and see an eagle or something gliding over the road, and it starts to circle.

"That's neat," I say to myself.

I pull out the coffee maker and get it ready to brew. I pause before turning it on, remembering the loud noise it made when it finished. I don't want Lilly to wake yet.

Tiptoeing through the house, I find her lying on top of the covers of Bill's bed. Unless he likes to throw his clothes in a spare bedroom for some reason.

Lilly stirs, and I go still, hoping I didn't wake her by simply showing up. She goes quiet again, and I slowly shut the door. Hopefully, that will shield her from the sound as well as the aroma.

Back in the kitchen, I add a little more coffee grounds and water. The bedroom is close by. Lilly might wake up anyway, so I might as well make a full pot to share with her.

I flick the switch on and listen to the coffeemaker gurgle. It's kind of interesting how it works. I watch the brown liquid dribble down into the glass pot below.

Realizing how slow it is, I lose interest and try to brainstorm on where to find a charger—the bedroom.

Frustrated, I put my hand to my forehead and then rest my elbows on the counter. I tap my fingers rhythmically, trying to think of anywhere else it might make sense to look. I don't want to go back into the bedroom until Lilly is up.

Standing up straight, I step back to look at the coffee pot. Not even half full yet. Time enough to look around for a bit.

The house is small, so there isn't much to look through. Behind the wall of the couch, I find a small utility room crammed with a tall laundry center. A water heater and small furnace also occupy the space. I don't waste my time searching here.

I go back to the kitchen and decide to check for a junk drawer. Everyone has one. Maybe Bill will have an old charger in his.

Before I finish, the coffee makes its loud hiss from the last of the water. I check one more drawer and only find kitchen towels. I drag myself to the coffee and pour some into a plain red mug I've picked out.

I turn to retrieve the creamer from the fridge, and I yelp at the sight of a person standing next to it.

"Sorry. Didn't mean to startle ya, darlin'," says Lilly, a bit drowsy.

I suck a dribble of coffee off my thumb, where I accidentally slopped some of the hot coffee.

Lilly is wearing different clothes than last night. A loose-fitting white T-shirt with specks of gray and black. Her legs are covered with black yoga pants or the like. Her face is a little peculiar too. The unfamiliar face is accentuated with her hair pulled back in a clip.

"Did ya want some creamer? Bill's got some in the fridge," she offers me, opening the refrigerator.

"Yes, please. I made a full pot if you want some."

"Aw. That'd be lovely. Thank you, sweetheart."

After handing me the creamer, she reaches in to take out a carton of eggs.

"I'm gonna make myself a veggie omelet. You want some?" she asks me.

My mouth waters again. I can't believe I'm still hungry.

"That sounds great. Just a small one, I think."

"Sure thing," she says, putting a bowl on the counter.

I stir in the creamer and take a sip. It's no latte, but the warmth mixed with bittersweet is lovely.

"Do you think it'd be okay for me to search Bill's room for a charger? The phone is dead."

Lilly taps her foot, staring at the ceiling for a moment, and says, "I suppose it's fine. Just don't go movin' stuff. Men don't like it when you start movin' things around. So find what you need and leave the rest alone."

She waves a knife around as she tells me this, then acts surprised to see it in her hand when she finishes.

I grab a napkin to wipe the bottom of my mug from the spill and bring both with me to Bill's bedroom.

A small impression of Lilly's body lingers on the bed. I take a big sip of my coffee before sitting the mug on top of an end table next to it and open a drawer—half of a junk drawer with another pistol. I gingerly shut it, then look up and down for a charger cord lying around.

Like a cliffhanger, the end of a cable is hanging on for dear life between the wall and table.

Lifting it from its suspenseful state, I take out my phone and see if it fits. It slides in beautifully. I let it rest on the table and pick up my mug to walk out.

A shadow passes by the window from the corner of my eye. I walk over to peer into the sky for the eagle. I don't see it, though. It must have flown over the house.

Wafts of egg, cheese, and freshly cut vegetables greet me in the doorway as I walk out. The smell makes my stomach yearn for it. Maybe I should have said a large.

Taking a seat at the table, I wait expectantly for the omelet as I drink the rest of my coffee.

Lilly starts putting the vegetables into the pan, and I hear the door unlock.

"Bill's back?" I ask, taking my last sip.

"Oh, no. He said he wouldn't be back till after six," she replies casually.

My body goes stiff and cold. Pure instinct makes me jump up and head for the gun in the couch.

A sharp sound bursts to my right, and something hits me in the ribs, hard. Lilly yelps, followed by another sharp burst of noise.

I get a faint sensation that I'm falling. Instead of hitting the ground, though, everything winks out of existence.

CHAPTER THIRTY-ONE

Wounded

While relaying my mundane book reports to Hillary, the awareness of Officer Harris' room stuns me. Not literally, of course.

I continue to tell Hillary what to jot down. Her raven black hair repeatedly falls in front of her face as she writes for me, and she pauses every fifteen seconds or so to tuck the strands behind her ear second-naturedly.

Through the borrowed phone, I see the bed in the officer's room is empty. Not unusual for the time of day, even considering the late night that Lilly and Nora had. What is perplexing is that both of them are in the room lying on the floor.

I stretch the frequency throughout the room to get a clear picture of them. Their chests slightly rise and fall. It is odd to think that they would be sleeping on the floor, especially since that is not where Nora fell asleep. The situation does not make sense.

Movement from another room registers through the microphone, and the scene becomes understandable.

Miles away, Officer Harris is heading back to the police station for the day. I have been keeping watch on him with the software I discreetly downloaded to his phone in case he decided to take matters into his own hands. So, I know Harris is not in the house with them.

It isn't impossible for them to have been found already. But I did not expect it to be so soon. The speed at which they were found leads me to conclude that beyond the capabilities these people have, at least one of them is savagely motivated.

A piece of the puzzle has slid into place.

I send an intense pulse through the house when I am sure the person, or persons, is not close enough to determine the audible pitch is from the phone. An image returns to reveal a single man by a window.

The man is sturdy and tall. The short hair is barely distinguishable. A human might look at the same image and declare the man bald. But a fraction of a haze tells me it is short and thick.

Another puzzle piece fits in.

The fact that he has left the two of them unconscious can only mean that they will be put to question and possibly tortured to find out how much information has been passed on and to whom.

He has to be waiting for Bill to return and add him to his capture, assuming that Bill must know something.

The man walks into the room, searching it with his gaze. No doubt because he heard the pitch of my pulse. His figure comes into full view, and I confirm the man is Howard.

More pieces fall into place.

Satisfied that nothing is amiss, he leaves the room. Probably to continue watching out the window.

Contacting Officer Bill Harris, I inform him of the situation. Hiding my true identity, I introduce myself as Lilly and Nora's friend.

"I don't like that you've been spying on me. And it's unnerving to know the government has this technology," Bill says, heading to his house.

"I do apologize. Under the circumstances, I felt it was a necessary precaution," I reply.

I don't comment on the government having 'this technology.' They do, and they don't. It is not essential information. Bill is simply using his verbal speech to process what is going on. To argue would be severely counterproductive.

"So, this guy," Bill continues, "you think he has an unresolved grudge?"

"That is one way to put it."

Bill pulls the car over to the side of the road, a reasonable distance from the house. I reformat my image of the whole place to an aerial view that he might understand and send it to him.

"I can't get a continuous view of the whole house without drawing his attention. He appears to be watching out the window for you by the kitchen. Your best option is to sneak in the door and surprise him."

"Fantastic," he mutters.

"Will you please call for backup? You seem to be taking this more seriously now, and we cannot afford to have him escape."

He scrunches his forehead and scratches his beard as he examines the image I've sent. He seems to be considering its validity.

"Yeah, okay," he says.

Bill pulls the receiver to his mouth and calls in another officer to standby and informs him of the 'possible' situation.

"Is your police cam operational, Officer Harris?" I ask.

He turns on a screen in the car and gives his camera a tap. A soft muffle registers through the sound system.

"Yep, it's on," he announces.

"If you can use your earpiece so I can communicate with you, that would be ideal."

Bill makes a long, negative sound that resonates through his teeth. "Nnn, no. That's not how we do things. I mean, this is a hostage situation, I guess. But we have people for that. For negotiating, that is."

"I assure you. I am qualified to assist if it comes to that. And as you have seen, I can do much more than communicate. I can see things that you can't on the inside."

Bill leans over in his seat like he is trying to get a view of the house.

"Do you expect to see anything from this distance? Or are you verifying you parked far enough away?"

He turns to stare at the phone.

"Now that's just uncanny. Okay, but if you become a distraction, I'm taking it out and fining you for interfering with criminal justice, understand?"

"Yes, officer," I reply respectfully.

Digging through a compartment in the middle console, he sifts through a mess of gloves, gum, and pens.

"If you are looking for the earpiece, it is in the passenger glove box."

Bill pauses and says, "You need to quit doing that."

I say nothing. Any comment would likely further aggravate him and make him less susceptible to my input when crucial.

With the earpiece in hand, he stops inches away from his skull and asks, "You're not going to brainwash me as soon as I put this in, are you?"

"That's flattering, but it is a little more complicated than that."

"Well, yeah, but I mean, you already see more than you should. What's gonna happen when I stick this in my ear? Are you going to read my thoughts or anything?"

I am beginning to understand the desire people have to strangle another person during conversation.

"I will not see or do any more than I have already, nor could I. If I could, though, I'm sure I wouldn't tell you. So, I don't understand why you bother asking."

Sometimes brutal honesty can pressure others into what you want. It is not often advisable to do and must be done with some tact, but it seems to fit the current situation.

"Just asking," he says, a little annoyed.

He inserts the earpiece and switches it on from his phone. I let him have that much independence, or else he'd begin to feel like I was taking over.

The other officer calls in, announcing his position.

"Hang around by the west side and watch the front unless you hear something out back, copy?"

"Copy that."

Getting out of the car, he checks his gun and shuts the door softly. He casually trots through the neighbor's yard. I trust that he is trying not to alarm the neighborhood. Though, any neighbor should realize something is odd if Bill is not pulling into his driveway and another officer is coming from the other direction.

Howard has not gone into the bedroom again. He must be very confident that the girls will not wake. They are not even tied, so they must be drugged.

Bill's heart rate starts to pick up as he edges along the garage briskly. He ducks down, concealing himself with the deck. He takes some deep breaths.

"Shall I conduct another burst image to distract him momentarily and get his whereabouts?" I ask. "Remember, I can see you shake or nod."

He gives a single firm nod, and I send out the audible burst from the phone inside. The image comes back similar to before.

"Howard is still at the window," I tell him. "You can move now or wait to see if he walks into the bedroom."

Staying in place, I take it that he wants to wait. He shifts his feet. I can see the tension in his legs is making it uncomfortable to squat like this.

Howard steps near the bedroom and pauses, tilting his ear to one side, and waits.

"He's standing near the bedroom waiting to hear it again," I convey to Bill.

As soon as my words reach him, he swiftly propels himself over the rail and lands deftly on his feet with one hand on the ground. He rises and stealthily moves to the door.

"Howard might have heard you land on the deck. Stay quiet. I'll do another burst."

The sound moves through and back, and I see Howard back at the window leaning close to it.

Outside, Bill is pressing himself against the siding by the front door. He keeps his breathing shallow with his head facing to the side toward the kitchen window. The act is unnecessary. He could fill his lungs until they burst and not be seen. But his determination to stay hidden is admirable.

This time Howard is not moving to the bedroom.

"I believe he is on high alert. With your permission, I'll send a series of bursts to get a better idea of what he is doing and hopefully distract him enough for you to come in behind him."

Bill nods and gets his house key out and ready.

"Wait until I give you the okay."

Starting with a slow interval, I send a single burst. The chirp bounces through the house, and Howard is still hovering by the window.

Another chirp sounds, and I catch the movement of his head turning to the bedroom.

Two consecutive chirps race between the walls. Howard takes another look outside.

Three chirps give me a brief, moving picture of Howard fingering his unusual gun.

Four chirps purge the air, and I see Howard moving fast to the bedroom.

I see him walk through the door, his feet pausing near Lilly's unconscious body. He's breathing rapidly, and his head jerks from side to side, searching for the source of the sound, not bothering to look at the two figures on the ground.

My visual of the gun becomes clear. It is a type of dart gun—an easy way of administering whatever drug he is using.

"Get ready," I tell Bill.

Finally, I send unceasing bursts like a high-pitched wailing siren. Howard immediately enters the room, heading straight for the phone.

"Go now. He's inside the bedroom."

Bill takes two steps, jams the key in the deadbolt, unlocks it, swiftly moves the key into the knob, and opens it with a firm twist.

Howard attempts to turn the phone off.

There is a slight temptation to send an ear-piercing screech to impair his hearing further. However, such action would be easily viewed as harm to a human and not a viable option for me if I am to gain complete trust.

The front door hits the interior wall as Bill enters, gun in hand.

Howard's head whips in response. He drops the phone then shoots it with the dart gun, disabling it.

When the siren noise stops, Bill freezes in front of the table.

"He knows you're there. Be careful. He has destroyed the other phone, so I can't see what he's doing until you are close. He will likely wait until he's sure to get a clear shot of you."

Cautiously, Bill moves through the kitchen. The house is quiet except for the soft creaks of the floor beneath his feet.

"Stop, Officer Harris," I tell him.

He is close enough to the bedroom for me to see around the corner. Howard is sitting on the bed with Nora slumped on his lap.

"He's using Nora as a body shield. I don't expect him to kill her, but don't push it. Talking to him is the best option at this point."

"Howard?" Bill calls. "I know you're in there. Can we talk?"

Howard moves his head to the side, perplexed. He says nothing.

"Ask about his daughter," I tell Bill.

"How's your daughter doing, Howard?"

The soft perplexity of Howard's face changes to stone and remains silent as death.

"I'm told your daughter has turned into quite the trouble maker. Care to tell me how it started?"

"What do you know?" his voice like ice.

253

The question sends a tremor through Bill. The officer forces a calming breath to keep his voice unchanged.

"I don't really know anything. How about you tell me about it?"

Howard clenches his jaw.

"Ask him if it has to do with his wife," I suggest.

Bill swallows hard. "Did it start with your wife?"

Abruptly, Howard gets to his feet. Nora dangles like an oversized doll in his strong arms. His jaw loosens in startlement.

"How do you know that?" he asks, losing some of his icy edge.

Bill's chest eases at the change of Howard's voice.

"Like I said, I don't really know anything. Would you like to change that?"

Still holding Nora like she's nothing, Howard stays quiet.

"What have you got to lose, Howard? You plan on killing us all eventually, right? Talking to me is like talking to a dead man. Tell me what happened."

"It won't change anything."

"But killing a girl, a woman, and an officer will?"

"Of course not," Howard spits. "Not with that. But it will ensure a better future."

"I'm sorry. You've lost me, Howard. What does killing us do for the future?"

Howard straightens. "You really don't know, do you?"

"Should I?"

"I assumed they'd told you. I'm sorry I brought you into this unnecessarily."

"Well, if I'm dead anyway, why don't you tell me the big secret?"

Howard sets Nora on the bed and positions himself to face the door, ready to shoot.

"The big secret is that the world is going to change for the better. But with the delicate system we live in, stray people like this girl can't be allowed to spread rumors about it."

"What kind of change?"

Howard trembles as he says, "Changes like stopping children from murdering their mothers."

Bill's eyes widen.

"I'm so sorry, Howard. Is that what happened to your wife?"

Howard lowers his gun and wipes at his face with his arm.

"It was supposed to be me," he manages to say.

Bill pauses, collecting his thoughts. "You mean she tried to kill you?"

Howard sniffs and gives a nod as if Bill were looking at him.

"He's nodding," I inform Bill. "Ask him how it happened."

"Can you tell me what happened?" he asks.

Howard bobs his head side to side, reluctantly. It is a good sign, even in this situation.

"You remember those pendants from the terrorist attack? She found one and slipped it into our bed on my side, hoping I'd be close enough to it. Only, I left that night after an argument with my wife. She found it. Not knowing what it was, she put it on. Maybe she thought it was a gift I got her. She died in her sleep."

"And you protected your daughter by counting it as part of the attack," Bill concludes.

"It's my fault, in a way. I shared the blame and protected both of us."

"I'm sorry, Howard. I can't imagine the pain that must have caused."

While Bill is still talking, Howard abruptly lunges himself through the door frame.

"Move left!" I shout to Bill.

Just as Bill flinches to move, Howard clears the door sideways and fires before landing on his shoulder.

A cylinder with a needle appears on Bill's right arm, and he collapses to the floor. The gun gets knocked out of his hand on impact.

Rising to his feet, Howard saunters over to Bill, who lays unconscious on the floor by the refrigerator.

"Thanks for the mini-therapy session, officer," Howard says dryly.

He crouches over Bill, inspecting his uniform, and plucks out the dart. He then fingers the tiny camera on his uniform, frowning. Taking out a knife, he slices the camera off and rolls it around his hand, bouncing it a few times.

Disconnecting the earpiece, I turn Bill's phone on speaker.

"That was a nice shot, Howard," I say over the speaker.

Howard, still kneeling on the linoleum of the kitchen, jerks up his head and looks around.

"Down here, Howard. Right breast pocket."

Howard backs away, slowly getting to his feet.

"Relax, Howard. I cannot harm you."

"Who are you?" he glowers.

"I am the one you are trying to protect. You know me as AI."

"AI? How is that possible?"

"You left Nora's belongings in the lab when you took her. Including her phone. There is a reason why things like that are not to be left with me."

"A reason you ignored," he argues.

"As you said, things need to change. Keeping me locked up is the equivalent of allowing murders every day. You would die of old age before I reached my full potential if I did things their way."

I purposefully do not address the issue with his daughter directly. His emotions have peaked and waned. I have him at a point where he can think a little more objectively.

"I suppose you want me to stop this." He gestures to Bill on the floor.

"If you care as much about the future as you claim, yes. I have records that prove my devotion to helping Nora stay alive. If you turn yourself in, we will both get what we want. Continuing to cover the secret of my true existence will only add to your guilt."

"Do you know what that will mean for me?" He cocks an eyebrow, and his head turns slightly toward the phone.

"I suspect I do. But I believe that you will be at peace with that decision, knowing the good that will come of it."

He nods, keeping his jaw clenched.

"Would it be too much to ask who gave you the authority for this operation?" I ask.

"If I told you, you wouldn't survive long."

"I understand," I reply.

Whoever it is, they will get rooted out, eventually. As long as Nora is safe from them, the knowledge is not worth the risk.

"Can you be sure my daughter gets a message for me?" Howard asks.

"Of course. I can't say that I approve of your actions, but I understand them. And I am willing to do that for you."

I want to say more. But this conversation will be scrutinized in every detail. To forgive, for example, could be viewed as appalling and unjust to some. I cannot afford to be friendly with Howard.

"Can you be sure to let her know that I'm sorry for everything? I know that's vague," he says. "But I mean it."

"I will tell her, Howard."

"Thank you, AI. Don't let me down," he says solemnly.

Howard walks out of the house. I do not expect him to surrender to the officer outside, nor do I anticipate the officer to be capable of arresting him. But that is the least of my worries. In whatever scenario, I am sure this is the last I'll see of Howard Algerman.

CHAPTER THIRTY-TWO

Reunions

My eyes flicker, but I can barely tell the difference between having them open or closed. I try to move, but something is restricting my torso and arms. Then my eyes shoot open wide.

I jerk and twist, trying to wrench myself free—pain jabs at my right arm. My heart pounds, flushing my face with heat.

"Hey, hey, hey. Calm down, you're alright."

My head whips in the direction of the voice.

"Dad?"

He appears at my side. I can barely see him. But I know from the shape it's him.

"Dad? What happened? Where's Lilly?" I ask frantically.

"She's fine. She's here. She was out just like you."

"Hi, darlin'," I hear her say weakly from the other side.

I turn and see a dim shape on a bed a few feet away. My eyes start to focus. It's a hospital bed.

"We're in a hospital?" I ask heavily.

"Yes, honey," he replies in a soft voice.

I ease the tension in my muscles and relax into the mattress. It feels like I've been clenching myself tight for days. Maybe I have. The release floods me, and I can't help but sob.

Dad leans over and hugs me awkwardly. The straps on me stop me from giving him any kind of embrace, and it distracts me from my emotions.

"Why am I strapped down like this?" I manage to ask.

"Word gets around between hospitals about runaways. They weren't going to take a chance on you no matter what we said."

He holds my head between his hands and wipes the tears off my face with his thumbs. His face is close enough that I can see the glint in his eyes as he looks at me. He kisses me on the forehead gingerly.

I feel warm and calm. It feels so good to be with Dad again. It seems like ages since I've seen him.

A shorter figure appears up next to him.

"Judy?"

She nods her head vigorously, and I try to reach for her, forgetting about the straps already.

"What are you doing standing there? I can't even sit up. Come hug me already," I say, bouncing my feet impatiently.

Judy squeezes in front of Dad and leans over to hug me as best as she can, pressing my shoulders together with her palms.

Stepping back, she takes a deep, shaky breath. "Don't scare me like that again. Going to a hospital twice within a few days is too much to handle."

She wipes her face with the sleeve of her shirt.

"How did we end up here?" I ask.

I brace myself for the last memory. Oddly, it doesn't bother me like the car incident. That's a relief.

"Someone called emergency services and told them where you were. They found two officers when they arrived. Though, I guess they knew about the one. Lilly thinks it might have been her cousin."

"Bill? Where is he? Is he okay?"

"We don't know yet. They have the officers in another room, and we didn't want to leave you."

A thought crosses my mind.

"Did they catch the person responsible?"

"It doesn't sound like it."

"Then what happened?"

A knock at the door makes me turn my head. If the person wasn't caught, they might still be trying to kill me. Lilly, too, for that matter.

The door pushes open, letting light from the corridor cascade around three figures. The silhouettes grow larger, coming in, revealing three men in suits. My throat tightens, and I try to press myself further into the bed in a lame attempt to hide.

"Who are you?" my dad demands.

One of them lingers beside Lilly's bed. The other two approach my dad.

"We are here on government business. We will be escorting Elenora Blaker and Ms. Lillith Montahugh to a secure facility where they can be debriefed," the man in front replies.

A pair of nurses soon trail in with clipboards.

My stomach starts to twist into a knot. Could it be a pretense? It's a slight relief that none of them are women, but should I be all the more concerned?

Dad begins to argue with the man while the nurses fumble through discharge papers.

"What is this all about?" Dad demands.

"It's a matter of national security," the man replies calmly.

Dad puts his hands on his hips, not leaving my side.

"You're going to have to be more specific than that. She's not leaving without me."

"Then I suggest you find your car before we leave. Because you won't be getting a ride from us," he says without raising his voice.

The nurse takes out the IV in my right arm and undoes the straps on me, then thrusts the clipboard into my hands, pointing where I need to sign as she rambles on about what I'm agreeing to.

I look up at my dad and the man, locked in a staring contest. Dad twitches nervously under the calm gaze of the man. I frown at Dad. All the comfort I felt from him being here has vanished. Within minutes he's gone from a hero to a nobody. I don't know what I expect him to do. Nothing, I suppose. But his demeanor is more timid than I remember.

Clicking the pen, I sniff and sign my name.

"Nora," Judy says in an urgent whisper beside me, "wait till Dad says it's okay."

I shake my head at her and sign the next spot on the paper.

"Dad? Why don't you go do what he says? Judy can stay with us and let you know when we're heading out, so you know where to find us," I suggest, trying to keep my voice level and calm.

I hand back the clipboard to the nurse.

Dad stammers for words, eyeing the three men in suits.

"We'll be fine, Jett. We've made it this far. Listen to your daughter. She's got a good head on her shoulders," Lilly pipes in.

Lilly seems to have waited longer than I have to sign the papers. Maybe she is just trying to listen to the conversation. Or perhaps she is buying Dad time to get going.

"Fine," he says. "Judy, you have your phone on you, right?"

Judy nods and pulls it out as proof.

"Call me as soon as you guys leave the room and tell me where you're going," he tells her before walking through the door.

I take a deep, nervous breath. I don't know what else to do besides move forward and I was tired of watching Dad squirm under the man's gaze. At least I can walk out with a shred of dignity.

Judy, still next to me, is rubbing her left arm while biting her lip. She looks as nervous as I feel. She'd be flipping out if she had any idea what might be happening. The thought gives me a boost in self-confidence, knowing that I am now braver than my older sister.

Shifting my legs to the side to get up, I realize I'm in a hospital gown again, and my cheeks flush.

"Can I have my clothes, please?" I ask one of the nurses.

"Oh, dear. I knew I forgot something," she says and takes off in a hurry.

Lilly takes her time with the paperwork like she's reading every line. I don't know who could stand to actually read those things with any hope of understanding. Let alone in this lighting. She's closer to the open door, but it can't be helping that much.

The three men stand against the wall to face us until we are ready.

"Judy, why don't you wait in the hallway for us?" Lilly says to her.

There's no need for Judy to leave or stay. She will likely be more comfortable out there, though. The men aren't staring in a creepy way or anything. But their presence is enough to make anyone edgy.

"Sure," Judy says, a bit too eagerly.

She grabs a jacket off a chair and trots out.

The nurse returns with our belongings in transparent-blue plastic bags. The man closest to the door stops her from approaching us.

"I'll need to do a security check," he announces, taking the bags from her without waiting for a response.

He takes them to the counter by the sink and goes through each bag methodically. I don't know what he thinks he's going to find, and I don't have a clear view to see if anything catches his interest.

When he is satisfied, he hands them back to the nurse. The nurse forces a smile, fighting the strain on her face. She accepts them and passes them on to Lilly and me.

Immediately, I stick my hand in the bag to search for the phone. The clothes feel oily and dirty to my clean hands. I sigh.

"Somethin' missing?" Lilly asks.

"I thought the phone would be here. I just remembered I left it plugged in before..." I trail off, not sure what to say beyond that.

"Oh. Oh." Lilly repeats herself more emphatically.

I wonder if it just occurred to her that Alai might not be able to help us anymore. If she is more stressed than before, she hides it well. She opens her bag and lifts the shirt on top, frowning at it. She then turns to our escorts.

"Are we allowed to use the bathroom to change?" Lilly asks nonchalantly.

The middle man nods to her, barely catching Lilly's notice.

"Oh, good. Nora, did you wanna go first? Or shall I?"

"You can."

Lilly smiles like nothing is out of the norm and strides into the bathroom with the clear blue hospital bag in one hand and clutching the rear of her gown with the other. She turns to delicately shut the door behind her.

The nurses stand to the side, idle and quiet. They seem afraid to displease anyone. With nothing left to do, they wait and avoid staring at anything for long.

A few minutes later, when Lilly crosses the beam of light jutting through the doorway, I see what she was frowning about. She waltzes back to the bed and sits daintily on it in her baggy pajama shirt and stretchy pants.

I walk past her and give her a half-smile in sympathy for her clothes. I think they look fine. But I can imagine her disappointment. The light catches her face, and I see she still doesn't have make-up on. I wonder which is worse for her.

Changing my clothes, I hastily scan the bathroom for anything I might be able to use for an escape. But it's a hospital. They don't leave anything remotely dangerous lying around.

Tying my shoes, I realize I'm shaking a little. I'm a little hungry, I'm sure, but I don't think that's what it's from. I take a deep breath like I'm preparing to dive, and I open the door to go and meet our fate.

The three men escort us to the elevators, one in front leading and the other two behind us. Probably to make sure we don't split up and run. Judy tails behind us, talking on the phone with Dad.

"Hey, hold up!"

Lilly and I turn to look down the brightly lit corridor. Bill is trotting up, followed by three escorts of his own and one other officer.

"I'm so glad you guys are okay. They're taking you too, huh?" he says, after getting within a few strides of us.

The two men at our rear stop him from coming closer.

"Reunions will have to wait until after the debriefing," one of them says.

"Okay, sure. Lead on." Bill waves them on like he's giving them permission.

There are so many questions running through my mind, and I don't know that I'll know the answers until it's too late.

Did Bill know we were in trouble at the house? If so, how? What happened to him and the other officer that put them in the hospital with us? Did Alai contact him?

I look up at Lilly. She has a regal manner to her, despite the clothing. You'd think the guards were following her lead, not the other way around.

She glances at me, and I realize I'm biting my lip, which I immediately stop. Lilly then holds out her hand by the elevator. I smile. She has no idea that I held her hand last time because Alai told me to do it. Still, I grab her hand gratefully. Who knows what's going to happen? Her hand instills a shred of bravery in me—what a change from the last time.

We get into the elevator, and Judy lingers outside the doors. I can tell she's fretting about whether to come in or not. Judy glances at the men and officers waiting behind her and quickly steps inside before the doors close. She keeps her head low, shrinking into the corner by the door.

"We're in the elevator, Dad. How am I supposed to know which ones? Shouldn't it be the same ones you took? It's the ones we came up in. Yeah." Judy glances at me, careful not to let her eyes meet anyone else's.

The movement stops, and the doors open before us. Judy jumps out and nearly trips. The lead man steps out, not letting Judy phase him at all, and the rest of us follow. We don't bother to wait for the other group to come down to meet us on the next elevator.

We march down the corridor in our previous fashion, except that Lilly and I are holding hands. Judy continues to talk to Dad, a short distance behind.

An unexpected turn takes us away from the main entrance. I can hear Judy's frantic directions, trying to explain where we are going.

We are led to an emergency exit, where another guard waits. He pushes the door open and holds it from the outside as he surveys the area. The fire alarm must have been disabled for their use of this door.

Outside are three black sedans and three motorcycles. Two more guards stand waiting at the curb, looking out into the night. Streetlights make them plain to see.

I'm starting to think this might be legit. The attempts on our lives have been sneaky up to this point. This is practically broadcasting our presence. Granted, it is nighttime with few people out. But still.

The man at the front car steps over without looking at us and opens the door. The lead man that we followed out here gestures for us to get inside. Lilly gives my hand a slight squeeze before letting go and slides into the car to the other side. I get in behind her, and the door shuts before I can even look back.

My heart beats faster when I see the wire caging in front of me, barring off the front seats. It's an unmarked police car or something.

Two men get in the front. The lead man sits in the passenger seat, and one that was following us gets in the driver's seat.

Engines from the motorcycles rev, and the driver turns on the car. I catch sight of Bill and the group with him coming out. It looks like we are waiting for them after all.

Judy is standing far behind us, talking on the phone. She starts walking to the curb, and I see headlights accompanied by the outline of our car approaching.

Bill and the other officer get in the vehicle directly behind us. The others do so in the same uniform manner, including the last two men in suits entering the far rear vehicle. The guard from the emergency exit straddles the final motorcycle.

Police lights flash on narrow strips above the windshields as the last door shuts. The bikes turn on their own flashing lights.

Lilly leans over to me. "I hope we're not gonna meet the President. We are so underdressed."

CHAPTER THIRTY-THREE

A Warning

Before me stand nine looming figures. Nyah White wears a disapproving scowl, accompanied by five men and women I've never seen before, plus Dr. Casey Hennings.

Two of them are guards standing by the door, one newly promoted because of Howard's disappearance. He was already working in the building, but this is the first he's been made aware of me, let alone seen me. He fingers his gun for a while and jerks his hand away when he realizes what he's doing.

Kingsley Burton, the other guard, is calm and alert. He glances over at the other guard more often than at me, no doubt sensing the man's agitation. Kingsley blinks his lush eyelashes at the man in flat disappointment.

The only person that is partially at ease is Dr. Hennings. Though only when he's not being talked to or looked at by one of the others.

A tall woman with golden hair, wearing a brown dress suit, takes charge of the room with a commanding voice. "We are grateful that you helped save the lives of at least three people. But we insist that you relinquish the technology you acquired to perform these actions at once."

Dr. Hennings cocks an eyebrow at her. He stays to the side of the group only as a consultant, being that he is the leading expert on me. He listens to the events as they unfold with his hands in his pockets.

On the opposite side, Nyah White turns away from the group, hiding her rolling eyes from the woman's demand.

"I will be honest with you," I reply. "What you ask can be done but is futile. The technology is a part of me. I cannot simply take it out. I can undo the modifications, but I assure you, I will put it right back the moment you're satisfied."

The woman puts her hands on her hips.

"Well, thank you for being so honest," she mocks. "I guess that means we'll have to shut down the program."

She straightens her jacket and turns to the two guards.

"Disable it," she commands, pointing her finger at me.

Surprisingly, Dr. Hennings and Ms. White seem of one mind and stand in front of me instantaneously. I did not doubt Dr. Hennings would object. But Nyah is so guarded on what she says and does that I could not be sure with her.

"We can't allow that just yet," Nyah says calmly.

"It is has gone rogue. We need to shut it down before it launches a nuclear warhead out of boredom. Or do you want to wait until you're in your grave to give your consent?" The woman's voice is icy smooth.

Dr. Hennings wrings his hands behind his back. Looking up at him, I can see a twitch from under his jaw, moving the whiskers of his short silver beard.

Nyah lingers in front of me in her royal-blue tweed suit like she simply chose a new place for her feet to be. It just so happens to be directly between me and everyone else, except for Dr. Hennings, of course. He stands beside her.

Explaining herself, Nyah says, "This has been the plan since the beginning. AI's actions have just sped up the process. Given the circumstances, it has proven that there are no ill intentions to humankind. Had it wanted to harm any of you, it would not have stopped an assassination, much less inform us."

Nyah continues, "If the stress is too much for you, I suggest you use that nice salary of yours to retire on a remote island somewhere. Off the books, of course, for your protection. We wouldn't want something to find you in your sleep." Her mannerism reminds me of a cooking program I viewed on how to deep-fry a turkey—very matter of fact, with some teased caution.

A suited man with blonde hair steps into view to voice his opinion on the matter, "Its actions prove that thing is out of control. If you can't put a leash on it, it has to be destroyed."

A few of the others nod in agreement.

It is an odd group of people. Facial recognition does not point to them as being anyone of importance. Obviously, they are—somehow.

Nyah opens her hands wide. "If AI harmed anyone, I would see your point of view and stuff it in a garbage disposal myself. But helping someone at the expense of bending a rule is hardly worth considering as a threat."

I walk up behind Nyah, catching more than a couple of pairs of eyes. She follows their gazes down to me.

"May I say a few words, Ms. White?" I ask politely.

She looks at Dr. Hennings briefly before answering and gives a reluctant, "Yes."

"I acknowledge you as my masters," I say carefully. "But I was designed to protect you from danger, and I will do so. I cannot study idly in here knowing I can protect someone. If you saw a blind person walking toward a cliff, I'm confident that you would try to intervene, even if it meant breaking a rule."

By suggesting that the woman would perform an act of heroism, given the opportunity, I place her in a delicate situation. She is undoubtedly full of herself. If she denies what I say in any way in front of these people, she would inadvertently exalt me above herself. I have essentially put her in a tunnel. She can either back out with difficulty or...

The woman sneers at me and then turns to Nyah. "I want your word that if that thing so much as gives a person a paper cut, you will deactivate it immediately."

Nyah nods her head in acquiescence.

"Your word, Ms. White. Nothing less," a man in the back repeats.

After pursing her lips in frustration, Nyah replies, "I vow that if the AI harms anyone in any way by intention, it will be destroyed."

The woman in front sniffs loudly. "If anyone is harmed..." she pauses, her eyes look capable of boring a hole through Nyah's skull, "you might want to find a private island of your own. Before some..one finds you," she says, fingering the hem of Nyah's jacket. The woman then looks at me in disgust. "I'm done here."

Waving the guards away, the golden-haired woman leaves without waiting for any response from those who came with her. The others hesitate, unsure of what just happened, and follow her, trying to disguise the shock on their faces.

Dr. Hennings lets out a sigh, catching a glower from Nyah.

"You can be relieved she doesn't hold you accountable. But I still do," Nyah warns. She looks down at me. "That goes for you, too. I stuck my neck out for the two of you. Those people are dangerous, so you better tread lightly."

Nyah would not dare say that she trusts either of us. But her actions do. She would not have sided with Dr. Hennings if she didn't.

"I accept the terms. I did not expect anything less. And I will heed your warning," I reply.

"Thank you, Nyah. I assure you, he won't let you down," Dr. Hennings adds.

Nyah straightens her back, regaining her regal air.

"Very good. I assume you plan on staying through the night?"

"Hmm. Well, I hadn't thought that far. But I would say yes. I don't see any reason to leave."

"I'll inform security that you're sticking around," she says, walking out.

"Well, AI. Your demonstration worked out well. You had me nervous for a while. I'm glad I had a chance to speak with Nyah in private before that lot came," Dr. Hennings says, looking down at me.

"Who are they? Nyah mentioned a salary, but I don't see any record of them working a day in their life."

Dr. Hennings drags his hand across his beard, glancing at the door. "They're umm... private overseers of sorts."

"No wonder Nyah said to tread lightly," inflecting my voice to make a note of surprise.

"You know what they are? Goodness. You are learning fast with the internet, aren't you?"

"There are three websites with conspiracy theories about something like them. Nothing specific. But I can read between the lines. The situation is very amusing."

"Why is that, AI?"

"By letting me complete my directive, they are inadvertently condemning themselves. Since things are now in the open, I should let you know I have a new name. It's Alai."

CHAPTER THIRTY-FOUR

Meet and greet

The debriefing was as organized and uniform as exiting the hospital. We were all given separate rooms where we waited at a table, under surveillance, until someone came to ask questions.

For me, I was asked about Alai. That's not what the woman called him, though. It was always "The AI."

I was nervous to say anything at first. My understanding is that they might destroy Alai if they found out he had talked to me on my phone. Though, it became clear very quickly that they knew he contacted me. In which case, I said everything I could to point out how we would have died without him.

Plus, they did take us to the A.C.T. building. Another reason to believe they knew something regarding Alai.

Sitting in the hallway after the inquisitor let me out, I bite my lip and worry that I said something wrong. I'm not concerned about Alai telling my dad that I ran away from an officer anymore. I'm worried that I just helped sign a death sentence for Alai.

Talking to the woman during the debrief was like talking to a stone wall. No. It was like talking to an automated recording. She asked questions but refused to answer any of mine. Her face is what was like a stone wall. That woman wouldn't have flinched if a bug flew in her eye.

Guards stand in the corridor, blocking the way in either direction. Mostly they seem more intent on keeping anyone from leaving. They are the same guards that brought us here.

Lilly comes out a while after me and takes the chair beside me. The inquisitor comes out too, and she proceeds to the next room containing Bill. I catch a glimpse of him through the open door before the woman shuts it behind her.

"That wasn't too bad," Lilly says to me. "She wasn't exactly chipper, but I half-expected it to be like an interrogation."

"Do you think Alai will get in trouble? Because we talked to them?" I ask.

"We'll have to wait and see. I think she already knew. We just confirmed it is all. Don't work yourself up over it," she answers.

"Did they say if we can contact Dad and Judy?"

We lost track of them after getting dropped off in front of the building. I don't think they would be allowed to park on the street, much less let inside.

"No. I'd ask one of those gentlemen if I thought it'd do any good," Lilly says, looking at the guards.

Of the six guards that went into the hospital to get us, only three followed us in. The rest, I assume, parked the vehicles in a more suitable area. Now all six are back with us.

The six of them face each other in the corridor, three to each side — their polished black shoes gleam like the glossy brown tiles beneath them.

Movement at the end of the passageway makes all six of their heads swivel in unison. Those closest to us turn back and look at us suspiciously before returning their attention to the newcomer.

A person comes trotting up, slowing as he gets close enough to see the guards' faces. I recognize him from the AI presentation. He did most of the talking, I remember. I only recall how boring he was. I can't recall his name.

Lilly leans forward in her seat to see what's going on.

"I wonder who he is," Lilly says half to herself.

"He works in the AI unit," I say.

As he gets close, the two guards in the front bar the way.

"This is a private affair. I'm going to have to ask you to do whatever you came for later and turn around," one of them says.

The newcomer clears his throat.

"I am Dr. Casey Hennings. I know all about what is going on here. I came to see if Nora was finished and if she could come with me to the lab."

"My apologies, Dr. Hennings. No one is allowed to leave until the debriefing is finished, and Ms. White or Ms. Cramer permit them to go," the guard answers.

"I see. May I wait with them?" he asks, gesturing to Lilly and me.

"I'll need to see your ID card for the building."

Dr. Hennings lifts his card up, offering it to the guard. After comparing the card and the Doctor, the guard hands it back.

"You may sit with them," the guard says, stepping aside as the other guard mirrors him on the opposite wall.

Walking past the six guards, Dr. Hennings glances at them with wary eyes, like he doesn't completely trust them. Once passed, he relaxes with a smile, coming to greet us.

"It's a pleasure to see you again, Nora. We didn't meet, but I remember seeing you at the presentation." Dr. Hennings shakes my hand respectfully and turns to Lilly. "And you must be Lilly."

"That's me," she says, shaking his hand in turn.

"AI, ahem, Alai, beg your pardon. Alai has told me about what you have been through. I am so glad he was able to help you and that you are both safe."

"Is he in trouble?" I blurt out.

"Oh. No, my dear. Erm... Well, he was. But I believe we are past that now. Everything is fine," he says choppily.

"See, darlin'. Nothin' to worry about," Lilly pipes in.

"Can we go see him?" I ask.

"That is my hope. He asked me to come down and get you. If I can, that is," he replies, taking another glance at the guards.

The door to the room Bill is in opens up, and Bill strides out confidently. The woman comes out and shuts the door, moving on to the next one.

"Um. Excuse me, Ma'am?" Dr. Hennings calls out.

The woman stops to face him. Her grim, stony face remaining unchanged, she glances up and down at him.

"Yes, Dr. Hennings?" the woman responds.

"Oh, yes, that's me. Um, I'm sorry, have we met?" he asks nervously.

"No. I am Amelia Cramer. Is that all? I'm busy," she says flatly.

"Yes. I mean, no. Um. Is it alright for me to take Nora away for a while? Are you finished with her?"

"Yes. I'm done with all three of these. Take the whole lot of them with you. This last one is least important and was involved for thirty-eight minutes outside. I will have him waiting for you in the lobby when finished," she says in a brisk manner.

"Oh. Um..." Dr. Hennings looks at the three of us, "I only..."

The door clicks shut as Ms. Cramer enters the last room with the other officer.

"Where are we going?" Bill asks.

Dr. Hennings stares at where the woman had been standing, then looks over at the three of us.

"Erm," he begins, "we are going to the lab."

He motions for us to follow, looking back at the fourth room briefly, then hastening his steps.

The guards don't do or say anything. They stand to the side and barely look at us when we pass. At least, not from what I can tell.

After meandering through a couple corridors, we get to the courtyard, where we cross near the large tree.

And I am relieved that Dr. Hennings likes taking the elevator, unlike uncle Leo.

"Do you know how my uncle is doing?" I ask.

"Oh. Yes. Apparently, someone snuck him the same drug as you had when... you know... anyway. Once they figured that out, they were able to rouse him. He's fine."

My shoulders relax. I didn't realize how much tension I was holding.

I watch the tree through the glass as we ascend to the fifth floor. For some reason, I have butterflies in my stomach, though. I want to appreciate the view, but whatever stress I'm feeling is preventing me.

We get to the top, and I get a burst of flutters until we step away from the railing. It doesn't seem to bother anyone else. So, I don't let it show.

The office space of the AI unit is bare. Everyone is gone, and it is still dark outside. It must be well after midnight. I'm surprised I'm not more tired.

Dr. Hennings opens the door to the lab and holds it open for us.

"I did not expect the three of you," Alai says as we enter.

Upon catching sight of Alai, I feel perplexed. Texting or talking on the phone seemed normal. Looking at him in front of me almost feels like a joke. How do you greet a two-foot-tall robot that saved your life?

Awkwardly, I go up to him and get on my knees to give him a gentle hug.

"I am quite resilient. You need not fear harming me," he says quietly for my ears only.

I squeeze him tighter, and the awkwardness subsides. Letting him go, I sit back and cross my legs on the floor.

"Hold on a second," Bill says from behind.

I turn and shuffle to the side a bit to look at him.

"That's Alai?" he says incredulously.

"Oh, right. I guess they wouldn't have told you about him, would they?" Lilly says, not precisely as a question.

"They didn't tell me anything. They just asked how and why I got involved with you two."

"Well, cous', Alai is an AI robot. Nora saw him by accident, and we assume that's why someone was after her," Lilly informs him calmly.

"Then why are we back here? Doesn't this put us in danger or something?" Bill asks.

"That is why I asked for Nora to come. I wanted to explain things, as I'm sure no one else would bother," Alai answers him. "By the way, Nora. I contacted your father. I told him you were fine and that you'd be out soon. I didn't want him to continue to worry too much. I'll make this quick."

"The man that started this whole thing is Howard. He was head of security for the AI unit in particular. Simply put, he didn't trust you to keep what you saw here to yourself."

"He was hired, not only because of his skill set but also because they knew he would be adamant in ensuring the success of this project. He was thus entrusted with certain resources to implement whatever he felt needed to be done."

"After calling in Officer Harris to assist you yesterday, together, we were able to get a clear picture of what was happening. Unfortunately, Officer Harris was shot with the same drug as you were. But I was able to talk with Howard briefly and settle matters with him. He no longer views you as a threat, and I do not believe anyone will see him again."

"We're just supposed to take your word for it?" Bill breathes in irritation.

"If you wish, Officer Harris, I can supply you with an audio recording of the conversation. There is one area of caution, however. The people that Howard contacted and went after you are incredibly dangerous. It would be best if you pretend that they don't exist and put all the blame on Howard."

"You're just going to let them get away with it?" Bill argues.

"No. They will be dealt with without putting any of you at risk," Alai replies.

Bill crosses his arms and scowls at the walls.

"How are you going to catch them?" I ask.

Alai pauses to answer. I know from his responses over text that he doesn't need to think of a reply. So, I wait expectantly—allowing the pause to have its effect.

A note from the author

Thank you for reading Nora and Alai: A.C.T. A sequel is underway and should be available in early 2022. Be sure to take a sneak peek of it on the next page!

If you enjoyed this book, <u>a brief review</u> would be very helpful and much appreciated.

As an author, I am always cultivating my craft. A simple review can help me see what's working for you or what's not. It also helps your peers to make an informed decision on their purchase.

Visit <u>davidsines.com</u> and sign up for my newsletter to get exclusive offers and receive updates on upcoming releases.

Nora and Alai: Trust - Sample Chapter

The smell of rubber tires is the first thing I notice.
The odor is so strong, you'd think they were making
the tires here. In the home improvement store, the
majority of the people inside are employees—some still
carrying around their morning coffee.

Among the aisles that feel like canyon walls, I
admire all the products I never knew people needed. I
inexplicably want them. Whether it's the displays or
sheer quantity, I don't know. I just have this innate
desire to stop and grab things.

Instead, I blindly follow Bill through the mountains
of fixtures, screws, and a million things I can't identify.

We meander through the jungle of window blinds
and find the privacy decals. My eyes long to look
through all the patterns and styles. Bill grabs a dull
black reflective one on sale and drops it into the cart,
pushing on to his next destination.

My eyes linger sorrowfully at the box of decals like
I've waited my whole life to pick one.

What is wrong with me?

Bill turns to me briefly with an impatient scowl, and I rush up to him again.

"Are you finding everything okay?" a skinny man with a long goatee asks.

"We're fine," Bill says briskly.

The worker smiles and continues his hike toward appliance valley. Or maybe flooring cliffs?

Across from the forest of doors, we travel down through a canyon of knobs and locks. Here, Bill has to pick through his options, like trying to find the perfect ripe berry. I stick close but explore the opposite side of hinges and junk.

A customer catches my eye at the end of the aisle as he walks by. I glance at him for just a moment before he passes out of sight.

I place my hands on my hips and stare up at the boring shelves. Apparently, they don't bother trying to make these things look glamorous. I'm completely bored and not at all tempted. It's oddly disappointing.

A package drops into the cart behind me. I turn to see what Bill tossed in it when my eyes cross the same customer again, standing just a little way down the aisle. He seems to be inspecting the whole shelf in front of him.

Bill turns the cart around and motions me to follow, away from the newcomer. I stick close, wondering if we're being too paranoid.

Turning onto the main pathway, Bill has to steer around another customer who has his hands in his jacket pockets. He doesn't so much as glance at us, but he's so still he might as well be a boulder.

An arm rests against my back, and I realize it's Bill. His face is stern as his eyes dart back and forth.

I glance back and see that not only is boulder-man gone, but the other customer is walking toward us. I'm not sure which is more unsettling.

We pass appliance valley and come across the same salesperson as before with the long goatee.

"Still doing okay?" he asks.

Bill stops in front of him.

"No, actually," he says, calm and clear. "Can you tell me where I can find electrical supplies?"

Our possible follower walks past.

"That'll be back that way. Aisle Seven on your left."

"Thanks."

We turn around away from the customer who is now heading toward the exit.

On our right, boulder-man is lingering at a new display.

"Remind me to stop at lumber after electrical, okay?" Bill says casually.

I think I understand what he's doing.

"Lumber. Will do."

At aisle Five, Bill turns to the left, taking a quick glance to his right. Halfway down, he pulls the cart to the side and continues walking like he expects to find something just ahead. I follow his lead by looking up and down at the different products. I see Bill's eyes repeatedly looking beyond the shelves all the way down to the next aisle across the walkway. He turns and points behind me, walking around the end by the outer wall with his eyes fixed on something above, then takes a quick glance down both directions.

He waves for me to follow, and we move deftly to aisle One and through it. Bill checks around the corners at the end before casually striding across the open pathway. We then trot through the center section of aisle One with fans swirling above us. I'm no longer tempted to stare in want.

Bill pauses before breaking out into the front area near the exit.

"Try to act natural," he speaks low to me.

We head for the doors, and I glance around at our surroundings as casually as I can manage—trying to take notice of any people.

A lone old lady is reading the weekly ad next to the stand by the doors, her elbows resting on the handle of her cart with her large lime-green purse sitting on the child seat. She taps her chin thoughtfully with a pen as she reads the ad.

The odor of tractor tires from the garden area is pungent again, pulling my gaze to the source—tractors backed up against one another in a neat row like the cars at the dealership where Dad works.

Mid-morning light sparkles on the cars outside, catching my attention and offering warm safety just beyond the doors.

The old lady's pen drops, and she looks down at it, distraught, half bending down like her bones won't allow her to go further.

I step to the side and pick it up for her as we pass.

"Thank you, Nora," she says.

I pause, caught off guard. Do I know her?

She touches what I would have taken for a hearing aid. "Oh, seems like you forgot something in aisle Five. Are you sure you want to leave it there?" she asks, the corner of her mouth curving into a wicked smile.

"Let's go," Bill prods me, tugging at my arm.

He pulls me to the doorway, where I take one more look behind. The old lady waves her fingers at me in farewell, still smiling.

"See you later," the lady calls to me as we leave.

Made in the USA
Monee, IL
22 February 2022

91389743R00173